8/99

MIDLOTHIAN PUBLIC LIBRARY

3 1614 00082 4079

W9-BIF-611

MIDLOTHIAN PUBLIC LIBRARY

Uncle Sam's Misguided

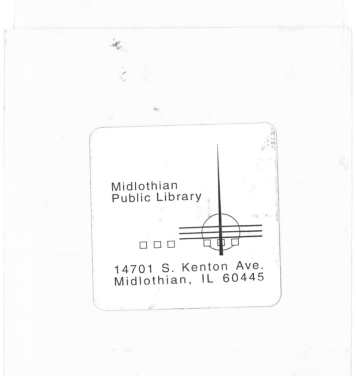

Midlothian
Public Library

14701 S. Kenton Ave.
Midlothian, IL 60445

GAYLORD R

Published in the Western Hemisphere by

Underwood Books Imprint of
Chambers Publishing Group, Inc.
Cleveland, Ohio 44119

Copyright © 1998 Michael J. Curran
All rights reserved.
First Edition. First Printing, October, 1998

No Part of this publication may be reproduced, stored in a retrival system, or transmitted, in any form or by any means, electronic, mechanical, photocopying, recording, or otherwise, without the prior written permission of the publisher.

Printed in United States of America

Illustrations:
Eugene R. Grynewicz

Cover and Book Design:
Abram Ross, Inc.
www.abramross.com

10987654321

ISBN No. 1-892509-49-0

MIDLOTHIAN PUBLIC LIBRARY
14701 S. Kenton
Midlothian, IL 60445

This book is dedicated to all United States Marines,
past and present.
Their blood, sweat and tears have made life better for all.
Even for those who don't realize it;
and for those who don't appreciate it!

And a special thanks to my wife, Cathy and my chidren
Kelly, Patrick and Amy
for putting up with me while
I concentrated on making my
dream a reality.

here are only two places on the face of the earth that make hell seem like a welcome relief. Marine Corps boot camp in Parris Island, South Carolina and Marine Corps boot camp in San Diego, California. Marines that took their basic training in California are fondly known as *Hollywood Marines.*

For those of you that served in the Marine Corps, you are well aware of what it took to make you a Marine, and you know there is no such thing as an ex-Marine. For those of you that have a desire to find out why your son, brother, uncle, husband, or father, who were or are Marines, think the way they do, please read on.

Marines are special people for many reasons. Marines do not walk under umbrellas, no matter how hard it may be raining. Marines do not put their hands in their pants pockets because they are not allowed to and because they don't wear pants; they wear trousers. Unlike their cousins in the Army, they do not salute indoors. They don't wear hats; they wear covers. There are so many different things that make Marines so unique.

In this book, Marines will share their accounts of what might seem like bizarre behavior to the outside world, but it was normal for a Marine recruit. At least by the time you finish this book, you might understand why your friend who serves in the USMC acts the way he does. For all the craziness . . . there is some logic, although it may be lost at times. The bottom line is that Marines need to survive at all costs. That's why they are trained the way they are trained. If a guy is going to break under pressure, the Marine Corps wants him to break in the states . . . not on the battlefield. The Marine Corps has a track record that speaks for itself, and it needs no fluffing up.

The entire structure of the Marine Corps is based on the discipline that is instilled in boot camp. I could never stress enough the importance of this training. However, like every other serious thing in this world, there is humor. I want to share some of the humor with you. Without that humor, many guys would never have graduated out of boot camp.

LET'S KNOCK SOME
SENSE INTO THAT GUY

We were sitting on our buckets cleaning our weapons like we did everyday. As usual the San Diego sun was out in full force beating down on the recruits. Then that dreaded voice, straight out of hell came bouncing down. "Private Wiggens…Private Biggens, get your sorry asses up here."

The entire company of eighty guys sounded off the drill instructor's request for the two guys that were about to get theirs. When a D.I. calls your name you know in your gut that you are about to be treated like no other human being has ever treated you. Of course, there is some suspect as to whether or not these D.I.s are really human.

Wiggens and Biggens were night and day when compared to each other. Biggens was a country boy…naive, shy and quiet. He did like to make little jokes now and then, but this was one time he wished he had passed on that. Wiggens, on the other hand, was a college graduate who by now wished he had gone on to graduate school. Both were from Indiana, but that was about all they had in common, except that they laughed at the same joke.

The drill instructor strolled toward the two screaming for them to bring their buckets with them. "You slimy pieces of shit will get somebody killed in Nam with all your giggling." He proceeded to have Biggens, the country bumpkin, step up on the bench and place the bucket over his head. Then he made Wiggens stand on his own bucket. "You hit this asshole on the head every time he laughs!" he screamed as he handed Wiggens a broom.

Biggens would have been all right as long as he kept from laughing. His problem was the D.I. gave him orders to laugh as loud as he possibly could. Then he continued to roar into Wiggen's ear, "And hit this bastard hard or you'll switch places with him. Every time he laughs you yell at him to laugh louder! Then smack the son-a-bitch!"

The rest of us continued to clean our rifles for the next hour with the California sun beating down on us. The only thing we heard was Biggens laughing and Wiggens yelling, "Louder!" And, of course, the sound of the broom stick handle whacking away at the steel bucket.

IT'S A BIRD...IT'S A PLANE!

We were standing in a company formation. That naturally meant you were at attention. That's not the most comfortable position to be in when it's around ninety degrees outside. To offset the thoughts of pain I was about to endure in the dental lab I began to think about home. I knew I would go home on leave in about three months. That seemed like a lifetime away. In San Diego, the Marine Corps Recruit Depot is located smack dab next door to the airport. I remembered landing there the day I arrived in California, but everything after that was a blur. As I was daydreaming about

home the roar of a jet taking off shook me out of my spell. I was still standing at attention. However, my eyes did sneak a peek at the colorful Southwest Airline jet.

My head never moved and I never relaxed my stand of attention, but my platoon commander saw the eye movement. "Pvt. Kerns! Front and center!" My name is Curran but that didn't matter, the chorus of platoon voices echoed the commander's order. They too, called me Pvt. Kerns.

With lightning speed I stood before my surrogate mother, father, all the nuns that ever taught me and God all at once. "Sir! Pvt. Kerns reporting as ordered! Sir!" I was so well trained that I was calling myself Pvt. Kerns.

"Did you see that God damn jet fly over my base, boy?" he screamed into one of my eyeballs covering it with his spit. I answered in the affirmative. "Good! Now go catch the jet and bring it back here! Now! On the double! Now!" he was still yelling as I was on my way down and around one of the biggest parade grounds in America. It took me twelve to fifteen minutes to make the trip that he expected of me.

When I returned I could see that he wasn't pleased that I did not have a jet in tow. "Pvt. Kerns, I gave you an order…now get your ass back there and get that air-o-plane!"

I took off again only this time I made sure I took about twenty minutes to fail at my mission. This apparently satisfied the D.I. because when I returned he allowed me to return to the formation and stand at attention.

Now I looked forward to sitting in the dentist chair.

FOOD FOR THOUGHT

If you were ever stuck in a desert then you could appreciate stumbling across an oasis. It's a lifesaver that will get you nourished and back on your feet so that you can continue on your journey.

That is exactly how most Boot Camp recruits feel about the mess hall. Unless they happen to be one of the people working there. But for the vast majority of guys the mess hall is a retreat from the heat, from exercise, and a chance to finally sit down.

Problem is you can't really relax. You have to walk through the chow line at attention; side stepping as some miserable soul throws your food on your tray. The good news is that you can eat all you want. The bad news is that you better eat everything you request.

There is no reprieve from the eyes or ears of the D.I. Actually it's worse because now there is a crowd of them walking up and down the aisles between the tables, always on the alert for any, and all, infractions of the rules. There is no talking aloud, no smiling, no laughing, no nothing. You just eat and breathe; that's it. Although, that sometimes becomes an almost impossible task. I might add that you are allowed to say grace to yourself before chowing down. That in itself is considered almost to be recreational.

One day I'm sitting there just about finished with my lunch. The guy across the table, and to my right, was full. Apparently his eyes were bigger than his stomach…he couldn't finish his food. There wasn't much, just a few morsels left on his tray. But he couldn't be seen dumping them in the garbage or he would end up doing a hundred push ups or some similar punishment.

I watched as the recruit skillfully made the scraps of food disappear into the empty milk carton on his tray. He was doing such a fine job disposing of the food that he never noticed the drill instructor behind him…also admiring the skill that the recruit was exhibiting.

In a voice so sweet the D.I. addressed the poor unsuspecting soul. "What ya' doing, Sweet Pea?" he asked.

"Sir! The private is finishing up his lunch," he responded hoping that by some miracle his deception wasn't noticed. No such luck.

Like a bolt of lightning out of the sky came the voice that would rock all the buildings in Chicago's Loop. "Don't you know that there are fucking babies starving all over God's earth. And you have the gall to throw away perfectly good food?"

The boot knew better than to make things worse for himself by lying. He knew he was dead meat now. So, he 'fessed up, hoping not to make a bad situation even worse. "Sir!"

He never had the chance to finish his response. The D.I. had instructed him to empty out the milk carton and finish off his lunch. Now that would seem like a reasonable punishment. It was appropriate for the crime. After all nobody was killed or anything like that. That wasn't good enough for the Marine Corps. This guy was going to become an example with a capital E.

The drill instructor began to reach every tray in sight and empty it onto the recruit's tray. "Start eating you, shit! Start eating!…God damn it!" The boot was chowing away. Hamburger scraps, potatoes, fish sticks, veggies (a well balanced meal), ice cream cups, and biscuits were making their way into the poor guy's mouth at record speed. Well, it looked like record speed. The record was soon broken when the D.I. decided to help the recruit out a little. He picked up one handful of squashed food after another and began to stuff it into the guy's mouth. He was choking, spitting, and gasping for air. The drill instructor, perhaps afraid that the recruit was going to croak on him, decided he had better help the boy out. The D.I. then picked up every carton of milk he could find and made the private chug-a-lug. By the time everything was over and done the private had every conceivable type of food all over his fatigues.

When he got up to turn in his tray…it was clean as a whistle. My guess is that he never again picked out more food than he could eat.

CIGARETTES CAN BE HAZARDOUS TO YOUR HEALTH!

If there is one thing that motivates Marine recruits in doing better than their best, besides unending punishment…it has to be the reward of having a cigarette. Lucky are the guys who happen to get a soft-hearted drill instructor. They may get five cigarettes a day. But the average is more like three smokes a day.

In 1968, the cigarette companies had just been forced to print the warnings on the sides of the pack of cigarettes. Anytime the drill instructor allowed the recruits to smoke one…they had to, in unison (even the non-smokers) recite the stated warning. "Sir! Cigarette smoking may be hazardous to your health!"

Then in a voice reminiscent of a dog owner speaking to his pet, he would say burn one.

And naturally nobody could light one up until they said, to his satisfaction, "Aye! Aye! Sir!" If this wasn't loud enough or not in perfect unison, then nobody smoked.

This particular day the D.I. decided who could put up two ponchos the fastest. Two ponchos, out in the field, equaled a small tent that perhaps a couple Marines could sleep in.

There were four squads competing for the bragging rights to setting up the tent. There were twenty men in a squad. When he gave the nod, everybody moved like a fire drill.

It was over when my squad finished erecting our poncho halves first. Not only were we not going to do the usual calisthenics for not winning, but he informed us that we could have a cigarette. We knew the other guys would eat their hearts out with envy.

We waited like puppies about to be rewarded for going for the first time on a newspaper. We wanted to enjoy our smoke at the expense of the other guys.

"All the ladies from squad one gather around here," he said in his most fatherly tone of voice. "Ya'll did a fine job here! And I guess ya'll want a cigarette. I don't think you should smoke in front of the other pukes." We naturally thought he was going to send us around the corner out of sight to enjoy our smoke. Remember, logic doesn't always prevail.

The drill instructor ordered us, all twenty of us, into the two poncho halves that sleep two. Once we were all in there, he lit the smoking lamp.

"Burn one, girls!"

They were right…smoking can be hazardous to one's health…when your in boot camp.

A LUNCH WITH ENTERTAINMENT

For the most part I scored very well in most categories during my time in boot camp. As skinny as I was, six feet tall and one hundred thirty-seven pounds, I ranked second out of eighty guys in the physical training.

The only area that I had difficulty was at the rifle range. That was not good for me because Marines, above everything else, are riflemen. If you don't qualify you would be the same as a castrated man. The Marine Corps wouldn't be too proud of you.

There are three categories of riflemen. The highest being an expert. The second level is a sharpshooter and the third is a marksman. Marksman will do, but it certainly won't put you in favor with your drill instructor.

My most trying day was on qualifying day with the M-14 rifle. You start out close and keep moving farther and farther back. Your last position is five hundred yards from the target.

My shooting was bad at the closer ranges so I wasn't looking forward to the five hundred shots. By the time you get down to the last shots from the farthest distance, you can expect to have some gorilla looking over your shoulder giving you encouragement such as; "You'd better make that bull's eye, Private, or your ass is mine!" I was never quite sure how he meant that. But no matter what he meant, it didn't sound good.

I was on my last shot at five hundred yards. I needed a bull's eye to get the lowest possible score to qualify. That was one hundred and ninety points. I sighted up with my rifle. I could feel this presence breathing near my right ear.

He didn't have to say a word…it was all in his breath. I squeezed the trigger and miracles of miracles I hit the bull's eye. I turned my head around expecting maybe a slap on the back for congratulations, but the D.I. was gone. I think he was disappointed. He had his heart set on doing me in.

The rifle range is located up north at Camp Pendelton. This is the only time, for two weeks, that a Marine recruit leaves the boot camp in San Diego.

Because we are up in the mountains it isn't feasible to go anywhere for lunch. So they bring sandwiches up to the troops in the mountain. The drill instructor informed us that we would have entertainment during our meal. Through the grapevine we found out that there were nine guys out of eighty that did not qualify with the M-14 rifle. I was glad I wasn't in their shoes, or rather boots. And I missed being in their boots by one point!

The sandwiches were passed around and just as we were about to eat the drill instructor made an announcement. "I congratulate all you men that qualified as riflemen for the greatest fighting outfit in the world." He seemed pleased to be speaking to us. "And as a reward we have brought in some entertainment…sort of like a Bob Hope Show."

Then three singers appeared and began to perform. They were three guys who failed to qualify on the rifle range. They were a trio that was very humiliated. But they weren't as embarrassed as the other six guys that had to pair off and dance cheek to cheek as the other three serenaded everybody.

It's amazing what one point can mean.

A GRANDMOTHER'S LOVE

I never knew my grandmothers. They both passed away before I was born. But I'm quite sure that they would have been proud of me being in the Marine Corps. And like most grandparents they would want to make sure that I enjoyed every bit of their love.

Private Murphy had such a grandmother. She was always writing him letters and had a lot of concern about how he was being treated. Now I don't know if Murphy shared all his Marine boot camp stories with her. But my guess is that somewhere along the line she decided he needed some cheering up.

Grandma was right. Because Murphy was having a tough time of things. He joined our platoon half way through our boot camp schedule. Apparently he was dropped from his first platoon. This is a terrible thing to happen to an individual because now you must go into a special group…get up to snuff…and then join another platoon.

What makes this situation so bad is that to begin with, the fact that you get dropped means that in some fashion you have failed as a Marine recruit. Depending on what your problem was you go to one of three places. If you're overweight you head for the "fat farm". If you're weak you go to the "skinny farm". If you are a discipline problem they send you to a platoon that is one step from going to the brig. In that place you are a prisoner.

These guys are issued two metal buckets and a shovel. They are sent to a place about the size of three football fields. It consists of sand…nothing but sand. In the morning they start at one end filling up their two buckets with sand. They run the length of the area and dump the buckets to make a sand hill. They do this all morning. By the time they break for lunch they have left a huge hole.

The Marine Corps says that anytime you see a hole you must fill it.

You guessed it. After lunch they do the same thing they did in the morning only now they dismantle the hill and fill the hole. They do this everyday for two weeks.

Getting back to Pvt. Murphy. He spent his time in the "fat farm". This is not winning points with drill instructors when they pick you up for their platoon. They see you as a liability that will slow their platoon down and cost them points in the overall platoon ratings.

It was a hot afternoon when we were in competition with another platoon for the honors of seeing whose men could all cross the rope bridge the fastest.

The obstacle consisted of three very thick ropes that stretch from one platform to another. Two ropes went just under your arms and the third one was the one that you walked across. From one platform to the next was probably fifty yards. The ropes were suspended about fifteen feet off the ground.

I was awaiting my turn to cross but I had Pvt. Murphy in front of me. He was scared and wouldn't step out onto the rope. The guys behind him made attempts to coax him but he didn't budge.

It was obvious that our platoon was quickly falling behind in the competition. It wasn't long before our platoon commander was standing below looking up in disgust. "Pvt. Murphy, get your candy ass across that rope!" he ordered. But Murphy wasn't going anywhere. He started to whine that he was afraid of heights. The other D.I.s were taking notice, and delight I might add, in the situation.

Now Sgt. Evans came bounding up the ladder. Surprisingly he never laid a hand on Murphy. Even more surprising was the fact that he spoke to him in a calm and decent tone of voice. "Murphy…you can do it, son…believe me. Thousands of recruits before you did it. They were scared too, but they made it. You can do it, boy," he encouraged the young trainee.

Apparently, the soft talk worked because Murphy scooted his way out onto the rope. First five feet and stop…then a couple of more feet and stop. He looked like he finally overcame his fear. When he was out about ten feet he froze like a rock. The knuckles were white and sweat poured down his face. "I can't!" he complained.

Once again Sgt. Evans came to the rescue. He spoke softly and again tried to get Murphy to regain his confidence. "Murphy, you're almost there…keep going," he instructed the recruit. Murphy went a few more feet but stopped again. Now he was out there fifteen feet from the platform. He was frightened to go in either direction. Our platoon was the laughing stock of the Company.

Sergeant Evans was losing his patience. Even the other boots were getting pissed at this humiliation. "I'm coming to help you down, Pvt. Murphy…OK?" he asked. Murphy nodded his head that he understood.

Then Sgt. Evans stepped out about three feet onto the rope. "You son-of-bitch, get off my obstacle course, get out of my Marine Corps," he screamed as he jumped up and down on the rope and swung the arm ropes all over the place. "Get down you bastard…you make me want to vomit!" Seargant Evans looked as if his eyes were actually popping out of his head. He jumped and swayed with all his might. At the same time Murphy was hanging on for his dear life and crying. But it took all of one minute for the drill instructor to knock him off the ropes where he fell onto the sand below. He didn't break anything, but he wrecked any chance he may have had to redeem himself in the Marine Corps.

He went AWOL that afternoon. My guess was that he was running as fast as he could back into the loving arms of his grandmother somewhere on the east coast where he lived.

THE HOMECOMING

We were still at Camp Pendelton. Only a couple of days left before we returned to San Diego. There are two things that Marine recruits do almost every waking moment of their training. One is clean their rifles. The second is field strip cigarette butts. This particular day we were cleaning our weapons. Of course we were sitting on our buckets. The platoon Commander, Sgt. Evans came out with a smile on his face. There weren't too many times I ever saw this guy smile. One of those times was at the end of basic training when he read off our orders. "Pvt. Kerns, you're going to the fucking WESPAC. That's western Pacific…that's Viet Nam!" he said with roar of laughter.

This time he was almost giddy. We knew something was up. He motioned to a couple M.P.s that were standing near the corner. "Ladies, today we have a surprise guest. I wanted you to see what becomes of somebody who is a quitter. Here he is…Pvt. Murphy." Sgt. Evans wasn't smiling anymore. You could see the fire in his eyes and could hear the contempt in his voice.

Murphy was embarrassed for sure. His face was always pointing toward the ground, afraid to look anybody in the eye. Sgt. Evans kept asking him humiliating questions, but the recruit never responded. The drill instructor said he was caught thumbing a ride on the freeway. The police caught him. When you have been wearing a cover on your almost bald head for weeks at a time everything gets sunburned except your head. When you go AWOL and get rid of the cover you stick out like sore thumb.

Sgt. Evans had Murphy standing in front of the entire platoon. He then had him put on somebody's back pack and run double time in place. As Murphy ran, Sgt. Evans started in again. "Pvt. Murphy, your grandmama must be a sweet old lady. She sent you this here box of salt water taffy from Atlantic City, New Jersey. I guess she didn't know that boots don't eat candy in the Marine Corps," he said as he opened the box and handed it to Pvt. Murphy. "Well, I'm a good guy, Pvt. Murphy…I'm gonna let you eat this here candy." Sgt. Evans was a man of his word.

Murphy got to eat his candy while he ran double time (in place) and was given a canteen of hot water to wash it down. When Murphy began to get obviously sick to his stomach, Sgt. Evans had him taken away. Nobody ever heard what happened to Murphy after that day.

AND HAVE A BLOODY GOOD DAY!

We had one week to go before the General's Inspection. That comes about two days prior to graduation from Marine boot camp. So for a week straight we got everything ready as a platoon and as individuals.

As a group they would score us on drilling with rifles, marching, and the total scores in the physical arena. Then on a personal level they would check our rifles, ask us about the Code of Conduct, the rules of engagement, and who the commandant of the Marine Corps was. Our bunks would be checked and our display of equipment and uniforms had to be just perfect for the I.G. If I had thought the drill instructors were picky before…that was nothing compared to getting ready for this inspection. One reason that it was so important was because many of the drill instructors were *lifers*. That meant that the scores received during the inspection had a direct result on the promotions of many of the drill instructors.

So we were having our final dress rehearsal. The Platoon Commander, Sgt. Evans, did the walk through of the barracks. He was checking each and every bunk display.

Eighty of us boots sat on our buckets studying the Code of Conduct while this inspection took place. If he called out anybody's name, you knew he was in big trouble. "Pvt. Bell!", screamed Sgt. Evans. Of course the chorus of recruits repeated his call. You could hear more yelling and swearing as the recruit entered the hut.

I was quite confident that my display was perfect…I had gone over it many, many times. Belt buckles were shined and turned in the right direction. My boots, shoes, and cover brim were spit shined to perfection. My dirty clothes laundry bag was hanging at the correct corner of the bunk.

"Pvt. Kerns!" Evans shouted at the top of his lungs. I felt a chill; I definitely had goose bumps of fear. I was perplexed as I double-timed to the hut. I knew everything was just damn perfect.

I arrived in what must have been a world's record for a sprint. "Sir, Pvt. Kerns, Sir!" I blurted out. I was bewildered. I was absolutely sure that I had prepared for this inspection perfectly. Because I wasn't allowed to move my eyeballs, I used my peripheral vision to check out my bunk. I had a glimpse of my dirty clothes strewn all over my perfect display on the mattress.

My attention was abruptly brought back to the platoon commander by his death defying scream. "Do you want me to go to jail, boy?" Besides shaking the only thing I recall was staring into his blood shot eyes and spit shooting from his lips into my face. Like a lawyer in court, he held up the evidence for me to see with his right hand. It was a pair of socks. Although they weren't dirty, they were in my dirty clothes bag. Instinctively I realized what they were and what crime I had committed. That was the pair of socks that I was wearing the day we stenciled our name with ink on all of our clothes. I forgot to take them off and mark my name on them. This oversight was on par with insulting this guy's mother on national television.

"Well….do you?" he literally spit out the words. Before I had a chance to respond his left fist came arcing around from the side. I saw it just in time to turn to see what it was. That was a grave mistake. Instead of getting clipped on the cheek bone, I unfortunately sacrificed my nose.

Besides feeling an instant numbness in my nose I also felt the thud of my head hitting the steel support beam directly behind me. I never saw stars like most people talk about when they get punched. But I sure did see lights… different colors and different shapes everywhere. I think it was at that point that I began to dislike the State of California. I know it's unreasonable but I able but I equate California with boot camp….to me it's all one thing lumped together.

The platoon commander must of had a twinge of worry about my condition. He perhaps was afraid that he broke my nose…miraculously he didn't. But the consoling words poured from his mouth. "Get your ass outta my sight, Puke. Get ready for chow," he said for the first time without yelling at the top of his lungs. "And, private, if anybody asks, you tripped over a foot locker like the clumsy son-of-bitch that you are!" I was shocked and still pissed off. I never had a drill instructor speak to me so nicely. Yet, I wanted this idiot to get his ass in a bind for a change.

We marched to the mess hall. I cleaned up my face a bit but left the shirt as bloody as it was…I didn't wipe anything off. The Officer of the Day spotted me in line at the mess hall. He inquired about my appearance. I may have been pissed off, but I'm not stupid. Getting this D.I. in trouble would have caused me more grief than I ever could have imagined.

"Sir! The private tripped over his foot locker, Sir!" I answered like a good little robot. He knew, and of course I knew, what happened. It was just another day at Marine Corps boot camp.

PARRIS ISLAND SOUTH CAROLINA

When God banished the devil from heaven, he had two places in mind to send him—hell or Parris Island, South Carolina. All things being equal, He chose hell only because it was farther away.

This place is swamps, swamps, and more swamps. The only residents there besides drill instructors and recruits are the bugs, snakes and other varmints that call the swamp home sweet home. If the critters or the D.I.s don't get you, the heat and humidity will.

Although Myrtle Beach is located in the same state…it may as well be a million miles away. It's said that nobody goes AWOL from this place. A boot is actually considered lucky if he is caught. Otherwise the swamp swallows him up.

MEDICAL MIRACLES

Ted Hordecky was the typical young man that wanted to serve his country. He couldn't think of a better way to do so than joining the United States Marine Corps. He would give it his all…the only thing he expected in return was for the Marine Corps to make a man out of him.

Ted arrived at MCRD, Parris Island, South Carolina, in May of 1973. Naturally, the very first place to visit after having your head shaved bald, was to get the new uniforms issued. After getting the utility uniform thrown in his face, he soon realized that he wasn't going to get the dress blues that he had hoped for.

After the recruits received their uniforms the D.I. called everybody to attention. He began to spit out what he expected the boots to do and how to act. He made eye contact with everybody, including Pvt. Hordecky. Apparently Pvt. Hordecky had some type of twitch that made him wink with one eye every now and then. Unfortunately for Pvt. Hordecky, his eye decided to wink just when the D.I. was glaring at him.

"Are you sweet on me, private?" asked the drill instructor as he put is mouth about an inch from the recruit's face. He replied in all honesty that he was not sweet on the D.I. "Then what the fuck are you winking at me for you bastard!" he screamed. Ted's head was spinning. He had no idea what gave the man that idea. Before he had a chance to respond to the question, the drill instructor was yelling in his face again, "What's your God-damn name, boy?"

By now the private knew enough that when you are asked a question you answer immediately and at the top of your lungs. "Sir, the private's name is Ted E. Hordecky! Sir!" Ted thought he gave such a sharp answer that the D.I. would be impressed with him and get off his case. But the response was so good that it came off sounding like Teddy Hordecky.

Ted didn't know what went wrong but he knew something didn't set right with this man because his eyes looked as if they were on fire. "Are you a faggot Teddy?" the drill instructor roared.

It was a day that private Hordecky would always remember. He never used his middle initial again while addressing a D.I. and, he learned never to wink again.

EATING OFF THE FLOOR

The washroom…you call it that and in the Marine Corps they will take your head off. Latrine…call it that and they will drum you out of the Corps and put you in the Army. In the Marine Corps there is only one name for the place that you do your business and that's the head.

Of all the new experiences that young Marines must endure, this is truly the worst of them all. At home people were used to getting up in the morning and heading for the john. In a leisurely manner, sometimes with the daily newspaper in hand, they would take care of the call of nature. The only thing that might have bothered them at home was that somebody else in the family might knock on the door and tell them to hurry up so they could use the room.

Picture yourself in this situation…the recruits get up at four-thirty a.m. They double time to role call and then they double time to the head. It's first come first serve, so to speak.

The lucky guy is the first one in because he will be the first one out. There are about thirty commodes in there. The first thirty people take their seats. Everybody else follows. Now there are four to six people deep in line waiting to use the toilet that is occupied. These guys are standing at attention anxiously awaiting your departure. The line starts about two feet from your face…what a greeting the first thing in the morning.

The overwhelming odor (that's putting it mildly) will get you sick for sure unless you have a stomach made of iron. If you were the fifth or sixth man in line you are a dead man for sure. I, personally, enjoyed the tear gas chamber more. Then it's off to breakfast! What a way to start the day.

Next to your rifle, the head is one of the more sacred areas of the Marine Corps. It must be because you take such good care of it. You scrub it, you disinfect it, you make it sparkle…everyday! You can eat off the floor.

In June of 1973, Pvt. Hordecky's company commander was having a barracks inspection that naturally included the head. He gathered all his charges around the entrance and they stood at attention. They barely moved their eyeballs for fear of repercussions, but they witnessed the most thorough of exams.

The D.I. was at the back of the head, near the last commode. There was a sense of relief among the troops because not a word was uttered by the D.I. during the course of the inspection. As he approached the last toilet, there was a shriek that sounded like it came from somebody suffering damnation in hell. "Somebody shit in my toilet! Jesus, Mary, and Joseph, some asshole shit in my toilet!" the Company Commander roared. Hordecky and the others knew they were in big time trouble now.

With his back to the troops the D.I. bent over and pulled the log from the water which seemed to splash all over the place. "If I catch the puke who did this I'll have his ass in the God-damn brig!" he screamed at the frightened troops. Then they went into a kind of shock when they actually saw him hold up the log from the back of the head and take a bite from it. The collective thinking at the moment was that this guy was a first class, genuine nut case.

It wasn't until the end of boot camp that the D.I. explained that he reached in the toilet with his right hand, but had a candy bar in his left hand.

WHOOOPS!

N o matter who you are or how good of a recruit you are, there will always come a time when you are going be on the receiving end of some type of physical punishment. Usually in the form of calisthenics. In most cases there isn't any set amount of exercise that you must do. However, most of the drill instructors have a uniform command to fit everybody.

The platoon was out running. That wasn't unusual because you run everywhere you go, everywhere. This particular day the group was running to the PT Course, that's physical training. They were about two-thirds finished with the three mile run.

Some people hate the running while others love it. They find it as an escape from all the other grueling events of the day. Private Hordecky was one of the guys who liked to run. As they were about to complete the run he had some phlegm in his throat. So he wouldn't start to choke he figured he had better get rid of it.

He turned to the right and let it fly. For kids, especially in little league, spitting is almost a sport in itself. So one can appreciate the flight, arc, and density of the "projectile". Pvt. Hordecky was pondering just those qualities as he watched it shoot up and, unfortunately, right onto the drill instructor's face. He had been running on the side and to the rear. But unknown to Pvt. Hordecky, the drill instructor decided to speed up a little.

It wasn't long until the Private heard the words, "You will P.T. until I get tired, asshole!" Ted spent the next hour doing push-ups, pull ups, and squat thrusts. After that episode, Ted always made sure there were no pedestrians in the way of his spit.

SOME PEOPLE ARE ALL THUMBS

In Marine Corps Boot Camp there are two things that will definitely bring your world to an end, laughing and movement of your eyeballs. I don't care how slight that movement may be…it will be detected and you will pay a price.

One big difference between the San Diego experience as opposed to the Parris Island experience is the bug.

In San Diego bugs are non-existent. At least to the point that they are not a problem for anyone. But they are so bad in South Carolina, that if a recruit is being stung, or about to be stung, they must ask permission of the drill instructor to kill the bug.

Being the understanding souls that they are, the D.I. almost always grants permission to kill the little bastard. The problem that arises is if the recruit misses and does not kill the critter then they are on the receiving end of some type of punishment.

Private Hordecky was being scouted by some unknown type of insect. He wanted to request permission to kill it but he wanted to be sure he had a good chance of accomplishing the mission. To fail would mean hell on earth. So he reconned the little varmint first. In doing so he had to move his eyes slightly. From out of nowhere came a screeching voice in his ear. "Who the fuck told you to enjoy the scenery, maggot?"

The private knew he was guilty. All the recruits know better than to ever attempt to excuse themselves from fault. They learn to accept and adjust.

Naturally the drill instructor's know that the punishment must fit the crime. Private Hordecky spent the rest of the day with his rifle hanging from his thumb. What that meant was that he had to open the bolt on his M-14 rifle and let it go home…on his thumb. Once he was sure (and believe me..he knew) that his thumb was firmly in place, he continued with his daily routine. The only difference from any other day was that he now had a M-14 rifle hanging from his thumb everywhere he went.

KEN JACKSON
SAN DIEGO, CALIFORNIA
SEPT-DEC 1957

THE FEEDING FRENZY

Other than what he had seen in the movies, Ken Jackson didn't really know just how bizarre Marine Corps boot camp could be. He found out when one of the other boots had received a care package from home. If ever there is one thing that is taboo in the Marine boot camp it's candy. And unfortunately, for the entire platoon, that is exactly what was in the mail for one of the recruits.

Ken and the rest of the platoon were in the sheet metal huts that dotted the boot camp. He recalled sitting on the floor while he was attempting to spit shine his boots for the very first time. The voice of doom and gloom came bouncing off the walls. "Get out here on the double…fall in you slimey ass pukes! Now! Move It!" screamed the drill instructor.

Like Ken, all the guys ran double time and tried to find their rightful place in the platoon formation. Tallest first right down to the shortest guy. Everybody was in their skivvies. What a sight to see. All these skinny bald heads lining up right next to each other.

Once the dust had settled, the D.I. eyeballed them all. "We got us a private here who received a gift in the mail. We all know that's against the rules…don't we ladies?" asked the drill instructor. "This here private was kind enough to tell me that he wanted to share his good fortune with all you other pukes while he does P.T. (physical training)" he said as he pointed to the recruit down in the dirt doing push-ups and counting out loud.

Ken could hardly believe his good fortune. He hadn't had candy since the day he left Chicago. The drill instructor was ranting and raving about anything and everything. Ken was hoping there would be enough to go around. There were an awful lot of guys standing there in formation.

"When I give the word, ladies, you will get yourself a piece of candy," he instructed the bodies that were standing at attention. "For those of you mamas' boys who are too weak to get yourselves a piece of candy—well, you girls will be P.T.ing your asses off."

Ken knew he had to make a mad dash for the candy box that was sitting on the chair just outside the drill instructor's office. He was far away but he felt confident that he could glom a piece for himself because he was very fast.

Everybody was waiting and anticipating when the drill instructor bent over and picked up the box. "Ready...go for it!" he yelled as he threw the candy all over the dirt and sand.

There were clouds of dust, arms and legs swinging, and all kinds of yelling and swearing. Heads were banging against each other. Ken ran most of the way to the candy heap, but probably dove the last six or seven feet. He landed in a tangle of bodies and caught a couple of elbows to the face. He grabbed for a piece and shoved it in his mouth. He was disappointed to realize that he was chewing on an empty paper wrapper that the chocolates came in. He didn't give up. He kept grabbing and fighting with everybody else.

When it was all over Ken got lucky. The drill instructor saw the piece of paper hanging from his lip and must have thought he had eaten a piece of candy. No P.T. for him. For two-thirds of the platoon, however, physical training was added to their schedule for the next half an hour.

When Ken thought about it later, he realized what the whole scene reminded him of. It must have looked like a school of piranha fighting for food in the Amazon River.

SNAPPING IN ISN'T A SNAP

As all good Hollywood Marines know, the recruits leave the friendly confines of San Diego and head for the hills to learn to shoot at the rifle range. It's located in Camp Pendelton, north of San Diego. One would think that this would be a welcome break. In reality it isn't the same old torture…it's different torture.

Before anyone gets to actually shoot you must spend hours upon hours of "snapping in". What that consists of is learning the various positions that one must fire from in order to qualify with the M-14 rifle. I might add that they are also the positions that you must learn to shoot from in order to save your ass someday.

At the rifle range, in those beautiful, but chilly mountains, it is not uncommon to wake up at 0400 hrs. The recruits do get to eat breakfast the first thing in the morning. Then they get to run off the calories by running double time up the mountains for a few miles until they reach the rifle range.

Then the fun begins. They learn to shoot from the standing position, sitting position, in the prone. The drill instructor teaches them safety and how to aim. How to look through the sights and how to breathe. And most importantly…how to hold the rifle.

You must get your left wrist wrapped in the sling very tight. Probably the only time you have to do this is when you are shooting in competition, qualifying, and when you are a sniper. Other than those times you're as loose as a goose when you are firing your rifle.

But during snapping in they make you sit, stand or sit in the position for thirty to forty minute intervals. All you are doing is holding your position, aiming and killing the circulation of your blood in your arm from the sling being so tight.

After a few minutes the weapon that might save your life someday begins to feel as if it weighs three times of what it actually weighs. Your eyes water and tears run down your cheeks. It's cold up in those mountains and your body begins to feel like it is paralyzed.

For Ken Jackson, he spent an eternity one morning up in those mountains. He had held each position for thirty minutes or more. His last position was sitting on the ground. He had his sights set on the bull's eye of the target. His eyes were watering and his arm was numb. He could feel cramps starting in various parts of his body. But, like a good Marine, he willed them away.

There was one thing that morning he couldn't will away and that was sleep. He was sitting in the position for so long that he thought the drill instructors had forgotten about him. He didn't dare turn around to see if they were aware of him. The moment somebody breaks their position, the D.I. will break them. So there he sat... motionless; except for the extremely heavy eyelids that he just could no longer keep up. Bam! They dropped and did not open up. Remember when you are cramped in one position for so long that when you change it is difficult to even stand up at first.

Ken didn't have that problem because before he ever stood up...before he ever woke up, he found himself tumbling down the hill like a ball. He was so stiff he couldn't immediately get out of the sitting position. He didn't realize until after he stopped rolling that the drill instructor had given him a kick in the back to help wake him up.

TRUTH IS STRANGER
THAN FICTION

In all my own experiences in Marine boot camp, and those that people have shared with me during the course of these interviews, I haven't come across anything quite as strange as this story.

Ken Jackson was half way through his sixteen week stint of Marine Corps boot camp. Naturally the platoon had its share of failures and successes. There are times in boot camp when it seems as if the platoon can do nothing right. Boot camp can be baffling…it may seem that every move somebody makes causes the entire unit cruel and inhumane punishment. That's the norm.

So it was a strange day for Ken and the rest of his unit when they finished practicing on the parade deck. As usual, there hadn't been a cloud to be seen in the San Diego sky. They had been going strong from 0500 hours. It was now 1500 hours (3:00 p.m. for you civilians) and the platoon had just finished drilling. Hours had been spent practicing cadence, the manual of arms, and a variety of snappy salutes.

The troops had been dismissed back near the barracks. The smoking lamp was lit. Ken and his buddies felt they did alright on the parade deck, at least there wasn't any exercising punishment that followed. They took that as a good sign. But when the smoking lamp was lit that early in the day, they knew they did well.

While standing around trying to sneak in that second cigarette, the Platoon Commander and one of his drill instructors approached a group of recruits. They snapped to attention and they were prepared for the worst. To their surprise, the two leaders praised them on a fine job of marching. As quickly as they arrived the two men walked away.

Ken and his pals looked at each other and just began to crack up. They had never witnessed kindness in Marine Corps boot camp. That's why this particular story is odd enough to write about. I never knew anybody that served in the Marine Corps that ever had seen such an occurrence.

THE PRIVATE COULD RUN!

Private Jim Keathly was a recruit in San Diego, California in 1972. He was one the fastest recruits they had ever seen. This guy could have run in the Olympic time trials.

The entire series of recruits marched in formation to the sand pit. This was an area the size of three football fields. To a thirsty, tired ass recruit, it may as well have been the Sahara Desert.

We were there to learn hand to hand combat…more specifically; to kill somebody with a choke hold. For days we had heard all the stories about this class. For instance…in training you naturally don't want to really kill somebody. So the idea was to simulate the situation.

Everyone knew that they would issue everybody an eight inch length of black rubber hose. This was to be the choke weapon. And we knew that they would tell us that in order to actually kill somebody we would have to choke back on the Adam's apple. But in this drill we were to put the hose between the Adam's apple and the bottom of the other guy's chin. Then you would wait for his hand signal (a slap on the body) to let you know he was just about ready to pass out.

And we also were well aware that they would use some poor soul as an example up on the twenty foot high platform. They usually would choke him until he did pass out.

Out of a couple hundred recruits they picked out a guy way in the back and told him to get up on the platform. In double time he took off for the platform. I can't remember a guy running so fast before. I thought, man here is one gung-ho Marine. But then he kept on running right past the platform and off into the sunset. The drill instructor yelled to some of the company guides to go get him. They managed to tackle him about two hundred yards away.

Until this day, I have yet to see a man run any faster than that recruit did that day.

MANY ARE CALLED;
BUT FEW ARE CHOSEN

Ron Howington entered Marine Corps boot camp in June of 1971 at San Diego, California. The weather in Southern California is always hot and in San Diego, there is never such a thing as a cloudy day. Well the sun was shining on Ron when he reached his unit at MCRD.

Some guys get picked to be the hut's house mouse. They are usually the guys that catch all hell for anything that isn't just right. Others are told they are to carry the unit's colors. Sounds like a nice job until one realizes that they are going to be the one that gets his ass chewed out for every little drill mistake that a recruit may make.

But Ron...he had the distinct honor to be the protector of the skull. The senior drill instructor had a ceramic skull. At least Ron thought it was a ceramic skull. His duties were to keep the skull clean and to protect it from harm or abuse. There were many things to learn while in boot camp but Ron Howington knew that his number one job was to care and nurture Frank. Yes, the skull's name was Frank. He never did say if he had to say "Sir" while addressing Frank. But every recruit knows that if somebody isn't a lowly private, like yourself, that you are to address them as Sir at all times. From the beginning of boot camp until his days at the rifle range...Ron babysat Frank everywhere the platoon went.

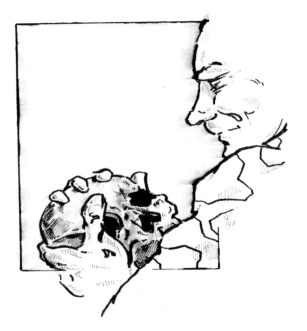

When graduation came Ron did not receive any award for the outstanding job he did. But he knew he must have done all right because the Senior drill instructor didn't kill him.

JET LAG?

After sixteen weeks of boot camp most people would be finished with any jet lag they brought with them from back east. However, there was one private in Ron Howington's platoon that wasn't so sure. He, at the very least, thought his body clock was screwed up.

The platoon had only three or four days left until graduation day. Although there was no slacking off with the D.I.s…with each other, the pressure was over. It was time for some good-natured fun.

There was a guy named Krussel. A likable guy that everybody got along with just fine. But the guys thought they would play a little prank on him.

Normally the lights would come on and people would jump out of their racks, get dressed and run out to formation. This was usually accomplished in a matter of two minutes…tops! This morning people jumped out of their racks and were yelling, "Get up…you're late, Krussel!" they screamed. He jumped out of the sack in double time, threw his utilities on, tucked in the shirt, threw his cover on his head, tightened up his bunk and was out the door. He had to be one of the fastest recruits in the squad.

Well this particular day he certainly was. He was the first private out there to fall in formation, he was the only one. What he didn't realize was that he was out there an hour early. He waited probably three minutes before he realized something was not right. He made his way back into the hut only to find everybody back in their racks sound asleep.

MARINES DON'T EAT DESSERT!

Bill Zick grew up in South Chicago, home of the steel mills that surround the southern edge of Lake Michigan. He was used to hard work. Hard work meant there was a payoff at the end of a job completed.

Bill had no illusions about boot camp. He was at Parris Island between World II and Korea. Like everybody else there he worked hard, probably harder than any other time in his life.

One day the drill instructor had him run to the mess hall a couple of blocks away with instructions to bring him some dessert. "Private, get your ass in gear. Go to the back door and tell them Sergeant Mills wants his ice cream. Move! On the double, boy!"

Private Zick took off like a bat out of hell. Like any good recruit he followed his orders to a tee. The mess hall Sergeant handed him a round three-gallon container of ice cream; flavor unknown, at that time.

Bill took his time heading back to the company area. He didn't want to fall or drop the ice cream so he walked rather than ran. Besides the heat was horrible in South Carolina in July. He felt he could use the rest.

"Where ya'll going there, private?" came a southern voice from the side of a building. Bill stopped dead in his tracks. He didn't know who was calling him, but he knew that whoever they were they outranked him. A drill instructor soon appeared. He inspected the Private, who was at attention as if he were a statue. "You got my ice cream, Private?" he yelled into one of Bill's ears.

"Sir, No Sir!" he yelled back thinking he would impress this guy with his snappy answer. "Sir, this here ice cream is for drill instructor Mills, Sir!"

The D.I. was now in Private Zick's face. His eyeballs looked like they were made of stone which meant that he probably had a heart to match. "That fat ass doesn't need any ice-cream, he needs more exercise, private", he said sarcastically.

Bill's hands were beginning to get very cold. But he dare not move a muscle. He figured Sgt. Mills would be ready to kill him because this was taking so long.

"Right face," the D.I. commanded. Bill did as he was told. "Left face!" Again the recruit complied. "About face!" came another command. Bill was starting to get dizzy. Between spinning in every direction and the sweltering heat, he felt like he was going to drop. But like all good Marines he dug down for that "something" that keeps you going when others give in.

The commands just kept on coming, one after another. This went on for about five minutes or so, but felt like an hour. Pvt. Zick couldn't stop thinking about the trouble he was going to be in for being late.

Suddenly the commands stopped. Bill was facing in the opposite direction of where he wanted to go. "You're a sloppy one, boy. Get at attention! Now!" the drill instructor screamed. "Now you just stay at attention until I tell you otherwise," he said.

By this time Pvt. Zick could feel the casing getting softer and wetter. A horrible thought crossed his mind. What if this guy wanted the ice cream to melt? After ten minutes, Bill realized that was exactly what the drill instructor had in mind.

After forty-five minutes the D.I. returned to inspect the recruit and his package. Once again the D.I. ran the private through his drills. He stopped long enough to take a peek inside the container. "Well, Private. Looks like your drill instructor is going to have to drink his ice cream," he laughed. "Now get out of here…on the double! Move it!" he shouted.

Private Zick reported in. He stood at attention as his D.I. look genuinely surprised at his appearance. Almost all of the ice cream had melted, soaked right through the case and on to Bill's uniform. It turned out to be vanilla….and the bees loved it. They were all over him.

"Go get cleaned up, Pvt. Zick." he said in a voice that almost seemed nice. As Bill about-faced and double-timed back he thought he heard the drill instructor yelling something about getting even. Bill was just hoping he was not going to be in the middle of it. He just wanted a change of clothes.

ARLINGTON HEIGHTS ILLINOIS

If any of the readers are familiar with Chicago, and its suburbs, they know that there are two kinds of people in this world…those from the southside and those from the northside. Growing up on the southside it had been driven deep into my brain they are definitely different. That may, or may not, be true…but when it comes to Marines there is no difference.

The first group of people to welcome me for interviews were the guys from the Arlington Heights American Legion. I could not have been more comfortable than if I were in my own neighborhood. Tony Handzel set up all the interviews for me. He let me use the large hall and tables for the interviews. Every time I finished with one guy, I would walk back into the bar and get another volunteer. I spent about five hours there. These guys made my job easy and lots of fun.

I want to thank them all for their patience and great stories. Even the Army and Navy vets were friendly. A great bunch of fellows indeed!

MONKEY SEE...MONKEY DO

Jim Levickis was another "Hollywood Marine". He described how the entire platoon marched everywhere they went. Whether it was to classes, physical training, dental, or to the head, they marched.

"We were only there about three weeks, one day when we had to go for dental check-ups. The entire platoon was marching down the street toward the dreaded Navy doctors. They could be real mean!" he stated.

He went on to explain that every time the platoon approached an intersection two privates were assigned to block the traffic of the street that the recruits were crossing.

"We came to a halt for some unknown reason. The platoon was blocking the intersection. Apparently we were going to be there for some time. I was standing there at attention and day dreaming about home in general and Rush Street in particular. I heard the drill instructor bark out an order. Sit down you asshole!" he related.

"Not realizing that he was only speaking to the guys blocking the streets I sat down. The next thing I see was the entire platoon dropping to the ground." Jim said. "When the D.I. approached me, he demanded to know why I sat down."

Jim was howling now as he attempted to relive the moment. "Sir, the private heard the drill instructor say 'Sit down, asshole', Sir." Tears of laughter were rolling down his cheeks as he tried to finish the story. "Sir, the private has been called an asshole everyday for three weeks, Sir! The private thought he was given an order, Sir!"

A SLICK CHARACTER

N obody except your basic bad ass street fighter particularly enjoys the pugil stick competition. Nine times out of ten you end up with some zombie that's four inches taller than you and outweighs you by fifty pounds.

That's exactly what happened to Scott Swanson. As he neared the front of the line, he counted down on the other line and knew he was going to catch his lunch. Scott could see that he was no match for the giant he was due to fight. He realized that a good portion of the fight is won by intimidation so he decided to stare down his man.

"So I give the guy my meanest look," said Scott. "Of course I didn't really have a mean look but I did the best I could. It did me no good at all. Actually once I caught my opponent's eye he seemed to get more worked up."

"The private glared at me," stated Scott. "That didn't bother me. He hadn't put on his head gear yet…then he did it! He blows his nose right into the palm of his hand and then he starts rubbing it all over his head and face. Jesus Christ, the last thing in the world I wanted to do then was get tangled up with this nut. Luckily for me it was over in a few hits to my head."

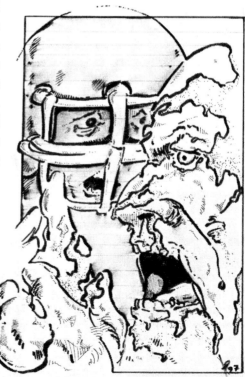

HAPPY NEW YEAR !!!

Sig Konopoteki left the Chicago Induction Center for San Diego during the week between Christmas and New Year's. When his group arrived at the recruit depot there was only a skeleton crew. They did get their hair cut immediately after getting off the bus. But the rest of the day they just pretty much sat in a building all day. There was hardly anybody on duty that New Year's Day. They spent the next few days just cleaning up while walking around in their civvies. They spent three days like this, not to mention being harassed and awoken at crazy intervals. In three days and nights they were lucky to get a total of six or seven hours sleep.

Sig recalled that on the stroke of twelve on New Year's Eve, things changed. The new full crew came on duty. For people all over the country the stroke of twelve meant celebrations and dancing, for Sig it meant that his nose was being pushed against the bulkhead and being screamed at," You fucked up my holiday you asshole!" roared a Marine as he barked one order after another. As he made his way from one receiving line to another to get issued all the bare necessities of life, such as clothing and boots, he felt like he had gone from purgatory to hell.

"I remember getting our first pay check," he said. The drill instructor made us stand in line backwards. They only let us keep about ten dollars, the rest stayed on the books. You only got to go to the PX once and could only buy toiletries. Anyway, even when they were handing us our cash we were standing in line backwards and had to reach backwards to get our money, we weren't allowed to look at the paymaster."

As bad as things get, all you have to do is look to others that have it worse.

"We would see the guys in CC (correctional custody). These poor slobs were out there in the sand all day. They had six guys down in a deep hole. Six guys were standing on one side of the hole filling it in with shovels' full of sand. The recruits in the hole had to shovel it out (to keep themselves from being buried) and build a hill on the other side of the hole. The drill instructors would give them a break though…every half an hour or so they would make the groups of Marines switch places," Sig roared.

MR. ROGERS?

If ever there is time that we look forward to it is meal time. In boot camp a recruit also longs for the moment he enters the chow hall. It could be that he is just damn happy to get out of the sun and heat. But often it is because he is famished. The Marine Corps puts out a good spread at breakfast, lunch and supper. Unfortunately for many recruits the chow hall can become a house of horrors. For Sig Konopoteki it was like home. He thought he was going to watch television after his meal.

"We entered the chow hall and went through the line and all that jazz. I didn't realize that you had to fill up every seat at the table. I didn't want to be stuck in the middle of the table, so when it was half-filled I filed in on the other side. I wanted to sit next to the wall," he stated. "That seemed reasonable enough…to a civilian. I didn't get a fork to my lips before Sgt. Rogers was in my face. Screaming and swearing at me; all I could hear were profanities. The only thing I actually heard was when he told me to report to the barracks immediately. That meant no food."

He jumped up from the table, leaving his tray, and doubled timed to the Sgt.'s barracks.

"I pounded on the door and yelled my introduction, 'Sir!…Private Konopoteki, Sir!' I wasn't sure what rule I broke but I knew he was pissed at something I did," Sig said.

The grin was coming on his face as he shared more of the story. "Now I was scared! Here comes Sgt. Rogers and he is pulling these skin-tight black leather gloves on his hands, making a fist!" (You could see Sig was reliving this moment in his head vividly. "I was shitting in my pants, this guy made Tyson look sick."

Sgt. Rogers was slamming one fist in the other hand as he spoke, "What the fuck is the matter with you? You piece of shit!" the D.I. screamed. Sig had every reason to be fearful. Nobody was around, they were all in the mess hall. This brute is strapping on the leather. Sig was thinking it was so the D.I. wouldn't leave any marks on his face. "You're smarter than all those assholes out there! Why would you go against my fucking program?"

One thing is for sure in the Marine Corps…and that is, that nothing is for sure in the Marine Corps. Just when you think all hope is gone…you get rewarded.

When asked by Sgt. Rogers if he was going to pull another stunt like that again, Sig responded loudly, "Sir, No Sir!" The D.I. appeared satisfied with the boot's response. Sig had an inkling that he was off the hook.

Sgt. Rogers approached the recruit face-to-face and eyeball-to-eyeball, "That's better, puke!" he said as he turned away. "Now you gonna' watch TV until the rest of the ladies get back from chow."

Sig couldn't recall seeing a television anywhere on the base since the day he arrived. He figured the drill instructors must have one in their hootch. Before he knew what hit him Sgt. Rogers had him pinned against the bulkhead. "Now assume the sitting position, puke!" the D.I. commanded. Sig was against the wall, he squatted as if he was sitting in a chair…two feet planted flat on the floor and his back against the bulkhead. He was instructed to put his elbows on his thighs and his chin in his hands. Rogers warned him, bigtime, he had better not fall to the deck.

So there Sig stayed until his platoon returned from chow. Sgt. Rogers came in…"Get the fuck out my hootch!"he barked. Sig could barely walk for the first few minutes after the punishment was terminated. But the good news was that he didn't have to watch any reruns.

CRIME AND PUNISHMENT

It is not unusual for one individual to simply dislike another for no other reason than the way you look to them. Unfortunately, that's a fact of life. When can this situation be bad? When the person that hates your guts is a drill instructor in Marine Corps Boot Camp. They can punish and humiliate you endlessly and there isn't a damn thing you can do to prevent it.

You can attempt to do better, be more gung-ho. You can shine above the rest of the platoon in every category and it won't amount to a hill of beans.

Case in point, Bill Marquette was telling of the time a D.I. came into the barracks one night. "If you have your rifle cleaned and everything under the sun spit shined, you might be lucky enough to have thirty or so minutes to write a letter home," he stated. "For no reason at all the platoon commander comes in, everybody jumps to attention like metal shavings to a magnet. The drill instructor was jawing on everybody in the hootch about how sloppy their drills have been. Actually, we had been doing quite well."

"We had some southern guy, Billy Bob or Billy Joe or something like that in our hootch. All three of our drill instructors hounded this guy. He was an alright guy, he didn't screw up any more or less than anybody else. But they hounded him constantly. 'Get your God-damn towels and assume the position!' the Sergeant commanded. 'Move it! Move it, you sorry ass mother fuckers.' Somehow we assumed the position. That was rather amazing because nobody really knew what the position was; we had never done this before. The position consisted of everybody holding their towels out in front of their chest with one end of the towel in each hand. You had to remain like that, at attention mind you. We knew what he was waiting for. Eventually somebody was going to drop their arms and get punished."

"OK, redneck son-of-bitch!" the drill instructor howled as he pointed to Billy whatever his name was. The D.I. waited until he saw the recruit elbows touch his side. "OK, Sweet Pea…sit your ass down on that foot locker, get nice and comfy until I get back."

Everybody stayed at attention as if they knew they were being spied on. The squad was in shock when they saw the drill instructor return with an ice cold can of Coke. Any type of treat in Marine Corps boot camp is a foreign sight. A Coke was like gold except that you probably would have an easier time getting your hands on gold than you would a can of soda.

"Get nice and comfortable there, boy. That's it…lean back and enjoy your drink while the rest of your hard working squad gets down on their elbows and toes! Move it! Move it, Ladies!" he barked with a voice that sounded like he was losing his voice.

Three minutes had passed…people were starting to lower their bellies to the floor. "OK, slimeballs…give me fifty! On the double!" the D.I. roared. Naturally everyone knew he meant push-ups until he got tired. After that it was squat thrusts until he got tired.

The Marine Corps wants you to train every moment of the day, and night, while you are in Boot Camp. So all these physical punishments were a blessing in disguise. The D.I.'s motives were certainly questionable. He was hoping everyone would get pissed at the redneck and collectively kick his ass. That never happened, everybody saw through his scheme. So in spite of the drill instructor the Marine Corps won. Their recruits were getting stronger and more disciplined by the moment.

THREE-HEADED MONSTERS!

Most people never get to see a three-headed monster. However, those who serve in Marine Corps boot camp do. I sat at a table with four guys from the Arlington Heights, IL post of the American Legion. Bill Marquette, Scott Swanson, Jim Levickis, and Sig Konopoteki all chimed in to tell their tales of the "Three Headed Monster." That's the Platoon Commander and his two drill instructors. They teach, they train, and they teach you how to survive. But in the process they make life miserable for you.

"In 1970 my platoon headed for the rifle range at Camp Pendelton, CA," Sig recalled. "They kept us in separate barracks, away from the regular duty Marines. I guess that was for our own protection. That way nobody could screw with us except the D.I.s."

Sig barely took a breath when telling this story. You could tell he was kind of reliving the excitement. "Their job is to harass you…make you understand that you are nothing. The three drill instructors came into the barracks one night and made us cover the windows with our bedding so the Commanding Officer couldn't walk by and see what was going on."

"I guess they do this to all the recruits," he said as he looked around the table to see if anybody experienced the same thing. "So the P.C. and his two assistants started screaming, telling us how fucked up we were and all. We were no good, just pieces of shit and all that stuff. Then they began running around like they went berserk or something…punching and kicking everyone they could get near." He paused as if he himself was stopping to catch his breath. "They told us, 'We aren't supposed to do this, it's against the rules…but fuck the rules.' They kept this kicking-ass crap up for an hour. We were all sweaty, dog-ass tired. One of the drill instructors told us we were going to be marched into the showers just like the Jews." There was a sense of bravo in Sig's voice. It was saying, it was bad, but we took it…we survived the worst they had to dish out.

"They marched us into the showers bare-ass naked. There was forty eight of us in the platoon. They ordered us to cool off and had the showers turned on ice cold. Jesus, it was brutal; there was nowhere to go. I remember starting to actually shiver. Anyway the D.I.s were swearing all at the same time. Their voices echoing in the shower," he pauses. Everybody could tell he was waiting to get on with the rest of the story. Every guy there could relate!

"The Gunny Sgt. yells, 'OK, ladies, time to warm ya'll up. Start playing leap frog….move it, now…faster, you girls aren't going fast enough.' I thought to myself these guys gotta be a bunch of homos," Sig laughed. "Forty eight naked guys playing leap frog in the shower? There were bodies falling all over the floor…the whole time these bastards are screaming at us. To this day I have no idea why they did that to us…no idea at all; except that it was regular fuck-fuck time for them. You know, their way of entertaining themselves."

"In Parris Island," Scott Swanson started to say. He wanted to contribute a South Carolina shower story to the group. "At P.I., you know it's very hot and humid. Anyway, they make us get into our ponchos and nothing else. Then they march us down to the showers, turn on the HOT water and practically P.T. us to death," he said with a look on his face saying he was glad it happened almost twenty years ago. "Push ups, leg lifts, squats (that must have looked great in the showers), and running in place. You think they would let us cool off with a cold shower? Not on your life. They didn't even let us clean up. We simply got dressed and headed for the obstacle course. Christ, we smelled like pigs."

IT AIN'T THE ENTRANCE
EXAM TO HARVARD!

In the late sixties it was real important to score well on your MOS (military occupational speciality exam)," Sig explained as he spun another tale of boot camp experiences. "You didn't want a fucked up MOS. Almost everybody in the Corps was going to WESPAC (Viet Nam). The only other duty might be embassy duty. Out of eighty recruits you might get one guy landing that job. We didn't get Germany or some other European tour…the Marines only had stateside and Nam to look forward to."

Sig was hoping to score well and land a cushy job. Instead he ended up in artillery. "I went in there to take the MOS test. They sit you down in those little cubicles…you know, the ones with the cardboard sides so nobody can copy your answers. On the other side of the table there is a partition, only six inches high, and it separates you from the guy across the table. Anyway, this guy is in there bored with the process so he starts to write on the partitions with his pencil," Sig was laughing again as he imitated the D.I. that caught the graffiti artist red-handed.

"You little dickhead, what the fuck are you writing on my God-damn walls for?" said the D.I.

He thought the recruit was going to lose his hearing from all the screaming that took place right up against his ear. The drill instructor made the recruit start erasing all the graffiti that had been on the walls for many years. All this was done with the tiny eraser on the end of the pencil.

"I want a clean damn classroom you fuckin,' moron!' the D.I. screamed. 'Hurry it up, boy, before I decide I'm pissed off!' With that the entire table shook. It didn't last for five minutes or even ten…the boot had to keep erasing for the duration of the test which was about an hour and a half or so."

"Is it any wonder I ended up in artillery?" Sig asked the guys around the table. "I was taking the most important exam of my life and I get this guy shaking the table like there is an earthquake hitting and the damn drill instructor ranting and raving almost the entire time. Hell, if it had been a normal test I probably would have ended up in the division headquarters or something."

WHEN NATURE CALLS.....

Some of us have excellent memories. We can remember the first fast-pitched league ball we hit. Maybe the first time we took the great step of planting the first kiss on the lips of a very special girl. Well, Sig recalled the first time he had to take a leak other than the scheduled trip to the head.

"Jesus, we had to run up to the D.I.'s hootch, stand at attention and rap our knuckles on his doorway three times. Not twice, not four times, but it had better be three loud raps," Sig said.

"I can't hear you!" the D.I. replied as Sig pounded on the doorway.

"Sir, the private request permission to speak to the drill instructor, Sir!" I

screamed. "Naturally I didn't scream loud enough for him and he made me repeat it. Christ, I gotta' piss so bad I thought I was going to burst.

After five minutes of him screwing with me he finally gave me permission. First I had to yell, 'Sir, aye, aye, Sir!' Then I had to take one perfect step backward and about face. Then I started to take off like hell. My kidneys were about to burst and I couldn't wait to get the heck out of there."

What would make matters worse is that the closest head was about a block away. Sig said that he had just taken a step and a half in the direction of the head when he heard, "Hold it you, puke!" The drill instructor wasn't finished with him yet. "Is this a God-damn emergency, turd?"

Of course it was an emergency, Sig thought to himself. Couldn't this jerk see that he was practically crossing his legs when he wasn't moving. "Sir, yes, Sir!" was his response to the King of Mean.

The D.I. glared with eyes that pierced and nostrils that flared like a raging bull. "Then turn on the damn siren, puke!" screamed the drill instructor.

"Picture this…Here I am running down the road, having to go so bad I can burst, and I'm twirling my arm in the air and going. 'Whooo, whooo, whooo,'" Sig recalled while laughing. "All I needed was one of those red lights flashing on my head."

NO FAILURE TO COMMUNICATE HERE!

Scott Swanson explains how he was greeted at Parris Island, South Carolina…it wasn't quite like the Boy Scouts.

"We arrived at P.I. about one in the morning. I knew what to expect. The D.I.s were going to scream and curse…get in your face. No big deal. I knew they had to do that because they had to deal with smart asses like me," he said. "Although most guys know what to expect it's still quite different when it actually happens to you. So they march us like cows into the second story of some wooden building. I guess for the sake of simplicity they were going to have to sleep in this place for the first night. There were one-inch thick mattresses piled all over the joint."

I couldn't help thinking that Scott was actually lucky. Many times they won't let you sleep for a couple days straight.

"I guess because of the hour they decided there wasn't anything to do but sleep. It was too late to even get hair cuts…and that's almost always the first thing they do to you. So all these boots are in line waiting for a mattress. The drill instructor is running up and down the room harassing anybody and everybody. I just didn't think too much of it…just the usual procedure," he explained.

"So we got this drill instructor yelling at everybody to shut their mouths, no talking and all that crap. Well, some guy next to me starts talking and a few guys were laughing at what he had to say. Wouldn't you know it, he starts in on me. Like I said, it was no big deal, I knew they had to try to keep everybody in line so to speak," he calmly mentioned.

"This guy is in my face cussing away with his southern drawl. I figured I'd play the game with him. Then BAM! He hit me so hard in my stomach that I fell to floor, it almost took my breath away," Scott said. "It was then, while I was down on my knees, that I knew these dudes were serious."

LET THE PUNISHMENT
FIT THE CRIME

During the sixties and seventies everybody that went into the military went through the big yellow Armed Forces Building on Van Buren Ave. Most of the people working there were doctors, who were giving the physicals, or members of the various branches of the service to process the papers and move bodies along from one station to the next.

There was some guy, a hard nose no doubt, who was being drafted into the Army. He was giving one of the soldiers working there a hard time. When he was confronted he pretty much told the guy to go to hell, that he wasn't in the Army yet and didn't have to take orders from him. The soldier looked at him and said calmly, "You keep this crap up and you'll find yourself in the Marines and on your way to Viet Nam!"

"You can't do that to me. I'm a draftee…it says right here I'm in the Army," he retorted. Then he continued to be disruptive for the next hour or so.

When everybody was finished with their physicals they sat in a room and waited for their orders. There were about fifty guys sitting in the room when the soldier came back with a stack of papers. He called off about three-fourths of the names and had those guys line up against the wall. Then he read off the remainder of the names. He had those guys line up on the opposite wall.

He looked at both groups and then addressed the smaller line up of bodies. The smart ass was the first man in line. "Fellas," he said with a smile on his face. "Welcome to the United States Marine Corps!"

The guy that had been shooting his mouth off looked like he was going to cry. He had good reason to….he was about to experience hell.

A GAS ATTACK?

"It was 1970, I figured they didn't hit anybody anymore in boot camp," said Sig enthusiastically ready to fire off another story for our entertainment. "We all go into a classroom, it was first aid or something like that. We weren't sitting down two minutes and somebody cuts one, loud, long, and very unpleasant," Sig laughed. "This Sgt. Harris just stopped everything and stared out at the class."

"In a bellowing voice he commanded, 'And the only thing I want to know is who the fuck farted?' With that a recruit admitted to the crime. He was called up on the raised platform by Sgt. Harris. The boot took about two steps up and came to attention. 'You think this is joke?' the D.I. screamed. Pop! Right in the mouth with a fist. There wasn't a sound in the class after that episode."

DON'T YOU DARE GET HURT!

Bill Marquette went into the Corps in 1966. Going to San Diego was a treat for him. It was the first time he ever flew on a jet. After landing at the airport and getting yelled at he was herded on to the bus with the other lucky souls there. He expected the usual…being verbally abused, with the idea that it was all part of the training.

"We went through the receiving barracks. Got the head shaved and stripped out of our civvies," he stated. Bill's platoon was issued their utility uniforms as they stood stark naked in line, moving from the shirt station, to the sock station and so on and so on. They were told not to get dressed because they would have to take showers before they could get dressed.

You could see Bill's thoughts were drifting back to 1966. "As we were ready to enter the showers all this screaming and cursing was going on. It wasn't just the drill instructors…every guy that worked in the place was cussing you out for something or other. It was amplified by the fact that the voices were louder and echoed more in the shower area. It was mass confusion," he said.

The boots were commanded to do everything in double time. Don't walk into the shower; run! Don't leisurely wash yourself with the bar of soap; do it at super speed. No time for drying off, just get the hell into your new utilities. Bill was on his way out of the shower when he felt his feet go sliding out from underneath. As he was descending he knew the floor was coming up hard. Then he felt his head smack the deck. "This sounds strange but I knew that I was out for at least thirty or forty seconds…I was aware of that fact as I was stretched out cold," he paused momentarily to attempt to think how he could articulate his feelings about what happened next. "I knew they were rough in boot camp. But I thought for sure somebody would help me up and make sure I was OK."

Obviously that wasn't the case. When the cob webs cleared he attempted to get up and at the same time was half expecting to feel a helping hand on his arm to get him to his feet. Instead the message was loud and clear, and, in stereo. "Get the fuck up you, puke!" screamed one Marine on his left only inches from his ear. On the right hand side came this message. "You useless piece of shit, you're holding up the parade! Now move it! Move it!" blasted another Marine.

Bill managed to scramble to his feet and exit the shower area. He knew then that he had better cut the mustard or they were going to chew him up and spit out the pieces.

MR. SANDMAN...IS THIS A DREAM?

During desperate times it isn't unusual for an individual to dream the impossible dream. Bill Marquette did that while he was near the conclusion of his boot camp. The drill instructor told them they were going to have a party after chow later in the evening. He was so tired that Bill actually thought the guy was serious about having a party. This didn't seem outlandish to Bill because he thought the platoon had performed quite well as of late.

Instead of returning to the barracks after supper the D.I. marched the platoon over to the showers. "Get in there, ladies! On the double!" he commanded his troops. A nice cold shower during the oppressive heat of August normally would have been welcomed except that these recruits still had their uniforms on. They naturally obeyed. "Give me fifty for the Corps!"

The startled troops got down and started their fifty push-ups. All the guys were glad when the push-ups were over until they heard the D.I. bark out an order for fifty squat thrusts; at double time. It was a relief to hear the D.I. finally order them out of the shower. Normally, eighty guys in soaking wet clothing would look rather out of place especially in sunny San Diego, CA., but not at the recruit depot. The D.I. then ran them over to the sand pits. "All right, girls, listen up it's New Year's Eve in August and I want a party! What do you do on New Year's Eve, ladies?" he questioned at the top of his lungs. "You get skunky drunk and fall on your ass on New Year's Eve, then you roll around in the gutter. Move it! You are drunk…fall down you stupid asshole!" he hollered out. "How come I don't hear anybody puking, pukes?" With that command many of the recruits began to feign the sounds of heaving their guts out.

When the drill instructor got tired, although it seems like they never do, the subhuman assembly was allowed to stop for a moment before they were double timed back to the barracks.

All eighty guys were now looking forward to a real shower, minus all the harassment. But to their surprise they went through the usual routine before hopping into their racks. Then the command for lights out came. The D.I.

instructed them to go to sleep immediately, not only did they not get a shower or change their clothes, but they had to sleep in them, sand and all. Welcome to sunny California!

PUTTING YOUR BEST FOOT FORWARD

Tom Clark came into the Arlington Heights VFW hall to share some of his first thoughts of Marine Corps boot camp. Tom looked like a hardened fellow that could take about anything anybody could dish out. But even he had to admit that the boot experience, at the hands of Marine D.I.s, was no picnic.

"I felt that boot camp was mostly psychological. Yeah, it was tough physically, but any kid in decent shape should be able to take it," Tom stated. I noticed what I noticed with most of these guys. When they first start to open up you can almost see their minds going back in time; like they are reliving the moment like it was now.

A smile began to sheepishly form on his face as Tom continued. "I recall our group was almost completely made up of guys from Chicago. We got there in early September of 1960 and the heat was brutal. We landed at the airport and stood around for two hours before a Marine Corps bus pulled up. It was like a yellow school bus except the color was different," he said going into great detail. "The door swung open and some guy, a recruit, was going to impress somebody with how gung ho he was. Anyway, the doors flew open and this guy runs up there and gets to probably the second step. The next thing you see is a foot slamming home into the guy's chest and he goes flying off the bus and rolls on the ground," he laughed.

That made me recall what one of my brothers, who preceded me in the Marine Corps, told me once. "Never do anything; anything, unless you are told to do so by somebody other than another recruit."

"Makes ya' wonder why ya' left home," Tom chuckled. "They messed with your mind. I'd go to sleep and have to pee three or four times a night when we lived in those Quonset huts. And of course the john was always two or three blocks away. You would walk there and always come across some recruit pulling firewatch (guard duty). By the time that asshole finished with 'Halt! Who goes there?' and all the other bullshit, the God-damn pee is running down your leg."

Tom seemed like he was ready to hit the road, and as had happened so many times before with other guys, he recalled more tales he wanted to share. "The drill instructor had us in a formation and noticed one of the recruits looking at the airplane taking off next to the camp. He called the kid out of formation, yelled and screamed at him for awhile and then made him spend the next four hours waving to the people on all the planes that took off from the airport," Tom recalled as he again smiled on the past. "I can still see him standing at attention next to the fence that separates the base from airport. He was looking up in the air waving to everyone that flew by."

Tom thought the Marine Corps had changed its ways after the infamous march into the swamps that took place at Parris Island, NC. in which six recruits drowned. "We had a corporal that was a real nut case…Schimmer or something like that. Anyway, he used to make people get into the thinking position. You know, hands on the chin, elbows on the ground, and toes holding you off the ground," he informed me. "Well just to show you how stupid this guy was. As you know you begin to get weak and shake before you fall to the ground. This nut would put a bayonet under the guy's belly. What an asshole. If the guy ever fell he would have been dead meat! Stupid, stupid, he was a dip shit!" he said.

Tom Clark noticed that I was smoking Lucky Strikes, the same cigarettes he used to smoke. "I smoked Luckies when I went into the Marine Corps. They didn't let us smoke for about two weeks. Everyday all we did was exercise and train. So everyone's lungs were cleaned out pretty good," he informed me. "Then one night they took us out of the huts and told us to bring our cigarettes with us if we wanted to smoke. Well it seemed like half the guys borrowed one of my Luckies. I bet, after one drag on that thing, that about six guys keeled right over. I mean they flat out hit the ground and passed out from those things."

Without missing a beat, Tom had another recollection to share. "We had this assistant D.I. from Texas. When he found out we could smoke he changed the rule. We could only smoke cigarettes that we rolled ourselves. He got a kick out of that because this southern boy could roll them with one hand. We had to go to the PX and buy Bull Durham or some crap. Well I couldn't roll a cigarette to save my ass. So whenever we got close to another platoon I would buy a few cigarettes from one of the guys. When we were gonna smoke I would roll one the papers around the Lucky and make it look like shit and all crumbly. And it worked…he never caught on that I was smoking Luckies," he laughed.

BIG MAN–LITTLE MAN

Jim Lavicus was an easy-going guy who seemed eager to tell his story of boot camp funnies. Jim served in the USMC from December of '63 to'67. He went through boot at San Diego…another Hollywood Marine.

He was already laughing as he began his tale. "You know how you have the three D.I.s? The good guy, the bad guy, and the platoon commander. Our bad guy was a Cpl. Larsen. This guy had to be the shortest D.I. in the Corps. He couldn't have possibly been over five-feet tall. I'm six-foot-one and I just towered over him. Anyway we had this kid, Patterson, a real nice guy, but not real smart and he was built kind of strange. He was a big guy but he was built like a bowling pin…real thin on the top and real wide on the bottom," Jim said as he continued to laugh. "Patterson wasn't very coordinated and couldn't do anything right. He had been dropped by one platoon after another until he ended up with us."

"Well, anytime we had to go drill or march they would leave him in the barracks so the D.I.s wouldn't be embarrassed by him in front of the other drill instructors. This one day they let him drill with us and he screwed everything up. Anytime Cpl. Larsen got mad at Patterson, he had a ritual they went through. The Cpl. would call Patterson up to the front of the formation and command that the oversized recruit pick him up under the arm pits and hold him at eye level. The D.I. would jaw him out and then told him to hold him to the left. Then Larsen would bite the kid's ear. Then Larsen would say go to the right and he would bite his other ear. I don't think it hurt him, actually I don't even think Patterson realized he should have been embarrassed. But this Larsen was a nut for sure," Jim laughed.

HOLD THY TONGUE!

I will always remember Tony Hansell as the guy that really started me off writing this book. He is a genuine nice guy. Quiet, friendly and unassuming. I had interviewed other individuals for this book before I ever met Tony. But I called him out of the blue and requested some interviews from the members of his American Legion Post in Arlington Heights, IL. They came through big time!

Right from the start of Tony's interview I had a sense that this was going to be different than the other guys' stories. And I was right! The tone was serious rather than the funny tales I had been hearing. Tony remarked many times how he liked, and enjoyed boot camp. He joined with two buddies from Chicago in January of 1966 and flew to San Diego.

Tony, to this day, is impressed with what the Marine Corps did for him. He grew up in the Corps; served in Viet Nam and became a man. He still believes it was quite a feat that the Marines took this city kid, who had never fired a weapon, and made an expert shooter out of him.

One thing Tony didn't mention about what the Marine Corps teaches… team work. But he learned it well. He rounded up the guys from the post to contribute to this southside stranger's book. They may be from the northside of the city, and I from the south; but we all share that common, unbreakable bond of being United States Marines.

Although Tony didn't come up with the humorous, belly-busting stories that the other guys did, he shared an experience from boot camp that might give some insight to the guy.

"One day the D.I. had us do something and apparently he felt I was straggling behind or something," Tony informed me. "He had the entire platoon stand in formation, at attention I think, and had me run around the group with my rifle held high over my head. The drill instructor said he was going into his quarters and that when he came out I had still better be running…and that rifle better be over my head or else the entire platoon was going to go running."

I watched Tony's face as the story unfolded. There wasn't any smile, but a serious explanation of what had taken place. "I must have run around the guys about four or five times and this big bad guy jumps out and starts screaming at me that I better make it or he would take care of me. He didn't have to tell me anything, I would never want the guys to be punished because of me. Anyway, I must have made two more laps and I was getting pretty exhausted, but not enough to stop or lower my weapon. Well here comes the same guy jumping out at me and getting in my face. I didn't let him get more than three words out and I belted him in the mouth with the butt of the rifle. He went rolling backwards on the ground. I never had another problem with him."

I thought Tony was finished but I guess he wanted me to see how funny life can be. "When I went to Viet Nam a year later," he continued, "and we were marching off to somewhere when this track pulls up and offers us guys a ride. I look up and here is the guy I had popped in San Diego with the rifle, and he greeted me with 'how are you?'"

A TRIP DOWN MEMORY LANE

John Reastat was from Naperville, IL. We met at a very busy truckstop just off of I-55 about 15 miles southwest of Chicago. The place was crowded and I was already there waiting for John to show up. I kept stretching my neck looking at every truck and car that pulled into the lot. I had never met John, only spoke with him on the phone. But I knew I would recognize him when he arrived because he was carrying that big red yearbook that they used to issue to the recruits after graduation from boot camp. After a twenty minute wait in strolled a guy with the book under his arm and eyes that darted all over the restaurant searching for somebody…me to be exact.

John had gone through boot camp at San Diego, CA in 1965. He sat down and it was like two old friends meeting. He couldn't wait to show me the yearbook. And I couldn't wait to see it because mine had been destroyed in a flood at my house years earlier.

We looked at the various obstacles that we had somehow learned to master some thirty years ago. The things that seemed impossible back then were history to us. Somehow the Marine Corps and the drill instructors motivated us to accomplish everything that they demanded of us in order to be called Marines. As I sat there and turned the pages, John looked on and commented about almost every phase of our training. It was like a friend showing you their old family album. And in reality the Marine Corps is like a family. Somehow you never forget names, faces, and events that took place no matter how long ago.

Jim seemed to know more about the guys in his boot camp platoon over the years. I only met two guys, by accident, after getting out of the service. The first guy he pointed to had been killed in Viet Nam. He didn't go into any details but I could see from the expression on his face that he really didn't feel like talking about it.

The second guy he recognized in the book was somebody he had continued to know in civilian life. He mentioned how he had introduced him to a business associate. Then he lost track of him. Later he found out the business associate had gotten mixed up in drug dealing. His buddy from the Corps had been into finances. Apparently the lure of money was too much. The guy ended up in prison for laundering drug money. It's strange, and unfortunate, how some people's lives end up.

When John was asked what boot camp experience stuck out in his mind he didn't hesitate for a second. "They had us write home, about two or three weeks before Christmas, to tell our families not to send any gifts or packages. My mother in her wisdom decided that I was in need of a fruit cake," he said with a laugh. "We were up at the rifle range in Pendelton when my fruit cake arrived. All I can recall was the three D.I.s had me in their quarters kneeling on the floor. They were stuffing the cake in my mouth. Then I had hot water to wash it down....and an occasional punch in the stomach. That wasn't to help me digest it...it was just part of the procedure."

SPECIAL EQUIPMENT ISSUE

I'm not sure who to give credit for this anecdote. The problem was that when this story came up there were about eight guys standing around talking. And I couldn't distinguish who brought it up.

The fellows from the Arlington Heights, IL American Legion Posts were gathered around the interviewing table. And one of them recounted "I was at Parris Island and everybody naturally had been issued boots. This one day the platoon next to us came marching by. Everybody had on sharp, spit-shined boots except for one guy. He was wearing snow white high top gym shoes. My first thought was that he must have had some kind of medical excuse for not having to wear boots. I remember wishing it was me. My feet were killing me in the heat," he said making eye contact with everyone at the table.

"The following week a guy in my own platoon had white high top gym shoes on. I was curious as to how he managed that. I was kind of interested in seeing if there was some way I could con my way into getting rid of my boots," he confessed.

"So I waited until we came out of the mess hall and asked how he rated those shoes," he paused as he started to flash a sly grin across his face.

"The guy tells me, he got caught masturbating! Anyone who is wearing gym shoes while everybody else was wearing boots, that means they were partying with themselves," the guy roared. "The place went up for grabs. One of the guys there had joked to his buddy that if it were him we were talking about…then the D.I.s would have had to get him a new pair of Air Jordan's every week."

THE OLYMPICS...THE WAY THEY WERE MEANT TO BE PLAYED

The next set of stories came from retired Msgt. David Head who now resides in the state of Arizona. He fought his way through boot camp in San Diego, CA in 1971. He was in Platoon 2069.

Platoon 2069 was out on the parade deck in San Diego. If you saw the deck and didn't see the buildings surrounding it, you would swear it was an airport runway. Drilling, drilling, and more drilling was the order of the day. David's group was new, so it wasn't surprising that the recruits looked more like a herd of cattle rather than a polished platoon of Marines marching.

When you're a new guy in boot camp and you see D.I. discipline for the first time, you can't help but think that whatever it is your witnessing, will one day happen to you before you graduate from boot camp. Well, almost anything.

The platoon had been halted and were about to go through the manual of arms. All eyes were forward and focused on the drill instructor. Then directly across the formation came a recruit streaking across the parade deck…yep, naked as a jaybird! And in hot pursuit was a foursome of D.I.s hollering, commanding, and running their asses off. Obviously this was one recruit who was not going to obey an order. The D.I.s ended up tackling him and carried him back to the barracks.

It was highly unlikely that this guy was going to end up with his picture on one of the USMC recruiting boards that we see everywhere. Within a week the drill instructors told Platoon 2069 that the streaker was mustered out of the Corps as a "psycho".

The year was 1971. At that time Viet Nam was winding down but there were still some troops being sent there. It is my gut feeling that this guy was not a "psycho", but somebody who wasn't taking any chances on being sent to Nam.

AIR MAIL

There are very few things that a recruit has to look forward to in Marine Corps boot camp. Graduation day and visitor's day are two that come to mind immediately. But during the daily routine of training, sleep, a shower, and mail are perhaps the most important events in a recruit's life. Lack of, or a complete absence of any of them can make life miserable.

In 1971, David Head and Platoon 2069, were residents of the new barracks in San Diego Marine Corps Recruit Depot (MCRD). His unit was on the second level of the building....the second deck.

"Our drill instructor would sit us down on the floor as he held mail call. Everybody, including the D.I.s know how special mail can be," David said. "He always sat us in front of an open window. This sergeant got pretty good at spinning around toward us and flinging the envelopes right out the window. If any one us couldn't catch the flying envelope...it was history; we did not get our mail."

That never happened to my platoon when I was in boot camp. I recall having to practically grovel for our mail. Many had to do physical training in order to get our mail...but at least we always got to read our mail.

"The D.I. was pretty good, he was fast," David continued with his story. "But it meant so much to us that we became very adept at catching it before it flew out the window forever."

SO, WHAT'S IN A NAME?

When people first arrive in boot camp most of their paperwork has their name on it. But by the time you meet your drill instructors almost everything shows only your first initial and your last name. Believe me you don't need a first name in boot camp. You can consider yourself lucky if they actually call you by your last name. When that happens I always thought of the guy as almost being the teacher's pet.

When I got David's story I thought this was "one for the books" so to speak. Actually it was one for this book. It was so typical of how things work for a recruit in boot camp.

"I arrived at boot camp and the first thing the D.I. did was look at my name, D. Head. With a voice that roared out from who knows where he asked me what the "D" stood for," David said as he told his story. "Sir, David, Sir!".

I could only imagine what was coming next…and I was right as David continued, "The drill instructor was all business as he determined that I needed a new name, 'From now on private, your new first name is Dick!' he commanded."

"Needless to say I was known as Dick Head for the duration of boot camp. Formally I was known as Pvt. Dick Head, but my friends would just call me Dick Head," David laughed. "I'm surprised they didn't put it on my ID at the graduation."

WHAT GOES UP, MUST COME DOWN

David told of the time his platoon was in the butts at the rifle range at Camp Pendelton. "We had to stand a rifle and personal inspection. The D.I. came by me and found a tiny, and I mean tiny, piece of lint in the barrel of my rifle. He started ranting and raving, swearing and carrying on. He, of course, made his point; he wasn't happy with my weapon. As he stepped away I was waiting for him to toss the rifle into my chest. Not this guy, he threw my weapon so high into the air that when it landed in the mud pit, the barrel was about five to six inches down in the muck. Of course I had to clean that sucker," he said. "At the time is was not funny. But today I can laugh about it."

David should consider himself lucky that there wasn't a bayonet on the end of it, if there had been, he may not be laughing today.

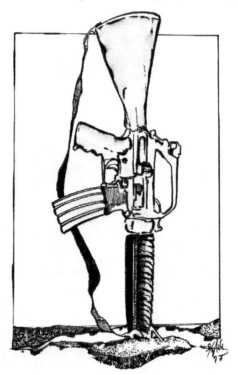

YOU ALWAYS HURT THE ONE YOU LOVE

I think there is something important to realize as you read David Head's stories. Here is a guy who ended up making a career out of the Marine Corps. He retired as a Msgt. He obviously was a good Marine and I'm sure he was an excellent recruit. The point that shouldn't be missed here is that no matter how well you do in your training…there is no escaping the wrath of these D.I.s.

"My drill instructor, and I won't name any names, had two pet punishments he just seemed to love to dish out," David explained.

"One favorite punishment was to put a pillow case over our heads and then use his cartridge belt with a canteen full of water to hit us in our bellies. If we fell down then we had to stand and get it again. This would continue until we (individually) could take a hit without falling down," David informed me.

"His second favorite punishment was to have us put our elbows on his wall locker in his duty hut. We would have to hang there for ten or fifteen minutes without falling off. He would just sit there and do his paper work while a private or two hung from the locker," David paused. "The more somebody fell off the locker, the longer the punishment would last. I only fell once!" said David with a sense of satisfaction.

EVEN MARINES CAN BE LIGHT
ON THEIR FEET!

"There was a feeling the drill instructor was drunk the night this incident happened. And as far I know it only happened once," David said with caution. "The drill instructor called a private into the barracks. The recruit came running at double time wearing only a towel. I'm not sure of the reason for this, whether it was punishment or simply let's screw with the private time," David informed me.

"Anyway, the D.I. made him get inside the metal locker. There was nothing in there except the recruit. The D.I. locked the locker and then put a can of sterno under the locker and lit it. (Sterno is the candle-like instrument that caterers use to keep food warm.) The only thing I really remember about it was the sound of the recruit jumping around inside the locker trying to keep his feet from burning," David recalled.

MOM AND DAD
A.K.A.
THE D.I.S

By the time I entered MCRD, San Diego, CA it was July of 1968. I had two brothers, Steve and Gerry Curran, who proceeded me in the Marine Corps. Neither brother attempted to encourage or discourage me from joining the Marine Corps. However, they made every effort they could to make sure I knew exactly what I was getting into and that there was no turning back once I signed on the dotted line. My mother and father, rest their souls, referred to the Marine Recruiter in Oak Lawn, IL, as "The Body Snatcher."

I recall the only burning question I had was if I was going to get punched around. I wasn't too fond of getting punched around after eight years of Catholic grammar school. My brothers told me I would only get wacked if I deserved it. That seemed acceptable to me because I had every intention of being the very best Marine that ever walked the earth.

Turns out I was neither the best nor the worst; I was somewhere in the middle and managed to be on the receiving end of only a few punches. Although one was a haymaker that nearly broke my nose, I managed to survive like thousands of other Marines before me.

Earlier in the book one of the guys mentioned the drill instructor's roles as follows: the good guy, the bad guy, and the not so bad guy.

In my case, (Platoon 1053 - July of 1968) we had a not so bad guy, the Platoon Commander; a bad guy to be feared; and a third D.I. who was a *real* bad guy. He had a deceiving smile and a sadistic streak in him. He seemed to enjoy every bit of punishment he doled out. With the other two, I always had the feeling that their punishments were given in order to make us better Marines. My three drill instructors were as follows; Ssgt. Evans, the platoon commander, Ssgt. Rouse; and Sgt. "Non-Descript". I can't recall his name now. But I can remember exactly how each one them looked and what their mannerisms were to this day. Although it is almost thirty years later I believe I could recognize any one of the three men if I saw them on the street today. It's a toss up as far as who had a greater impact on my life…the D.I.'s or the nuns in grammar school. It's just two damn close to call.

THE LES & LEE SHOW
NAPERVILLE, IL

This was the day I had been waiting for. I wanted to see what drill instructors were like in real life. In all my years after getting out of the Marine Corps I had yet to ever come across anyone that had been a Marine Corps D.I.

I met Les Kenny through a friend at work. We played phone tag for what seemed like months. Then we finally made a date and time to meet. There was a bonus. Les' good friend, and former D.I. Lee Weber, was coming in for a few days to visit. I was delighted to say the least.

Les Kenny's stint with the Marine Corps was from February 1970 until June of 1990. He retired as a Msgt. Les had been a D.I. at Parris Island, S.C.

Lee's career in the Corps, was from 1970 until 1992. He retired as a 1stSgt and had been a D.I. at both Parris Island, SC and San Diego, CA.

We met at a noisy canteena in the Chicago suburb of Naperville, IL. It is a well to do suburb located about 25 miles southwest of Chicago. When I met these guys I was taken back by the contrast between them. Les is a fellow about six feet tall and rather husky. He is an out-going, friendly guy with a very noticeable laugh to match his sense of humor. You couldn't meet a friendlier person. However, I had a sense about him that he was not one to be crossed. For all the easy going attitude he had, you could tell that when it was time for business he could be very focused and right to the point. Lee, however, seemed quite different. When I first met him I don't think he knew what to expect of me. He appeared to be rather cautious. But he lightened up after just a few minutes. Actually he was the first to get the ball rolling by sharing the first D.I. story. As large as Les was, Lee was short. He claimed that when he was a drill instructor, that he was, at that time, the shortest drill instructor in the Marine Corps. Lee was the type of person that you could tell, right off the bat, would be very proficient in whatever it was that he did. Turns out he is a teacher, and runs the ROTC at a high school in Waterbury, CT. I had been slightly concerned about how I might be received by these guys. After all, they were career Marines that had put in the twenty years to retire. And here I was, a two year enlistee. I did my training, school, and a year in Viet Nam and was gone. But those fears were gone. We were all Marines at one time or another and that's all that mattered. I find that true with almost anyone I meet that had been in the Marine Corps. Your MOSs may have been different and some never even went overseas, but it didn't matter. There was that Marine blood in you and that would never change.

.....AND THEN THERE IS THE MARINE CORPS WAY...

"And then there was Pvt. Craft," Lee Weber said matter-of-factly. "We were up at Edson Range, in Camp Pendelton. The senior drill instructor came up to me and told me that we were going to have a General's Inspection the following day. So we field-dayed and got ready for the inspection. The next day we were up at the rifle range and my platoon commander, (I was a junior D.I.), came up to me and said we had failed the inspection. I was stunned, I said that was impossible...no way! But he said we failed and I asked him why."

Les was beginning to smile, almost laugh. I had a feeling he had heard this story before. Either that or he instinctively knew, being a drill instructor, that it had to be something good.

"In the barracks we had laundry bags that hung on the end of the racks. Apparently, the female Lieutenant Colonel, that accompanied the General smelled something. After snooping around they isolated the smell down to a particular rack; Pvt. Craft's. So she sniffed around and found that it was coming from Pvt. Craft's laundry bag," Lee said with a hint of a smile for the first time. I could tell now that Les knew exactly what was coming because he seemed to be holding back from all out laughter. "So they opened Pvt. Craft's laundry bag, which was tied to the end of the rack, and found, I'll say, soiled underwear in his bag," Lee said without smiling this time. To a D.I. this is serious business. How do they explain to their superiors that one of their men crapped in his clothes?

Lee continued with his story. "I was out around the three-hundred-yard line when I found out why we failed from the senior D.I. I went over to Pvt.

Craft, who was a non-shooter on the firing line. I went over to him and laid down beside him to find out what had happened…and then I smelled something. Turns out Pvt. Craft had crapped in his drawers," Lee paused. I could only imagine that he must have thought at the time why is this happening to me?

"I told him to cease firing and get off the firing line. We walked him over to the tunnel. There was a tunnel between the ranges. We got in there and I told him to drop his drawers. He dropped his drawers and there it was…he had soiled his drawers! Needless to say we punished him," Lee informed us.

"That night I had the duty in the barracks. I called lights out and all was quiet. Then about an hour after lights out the fire watch came into the duty office and said 'Don't walk out the door,' I asked him why. He said, 'Pvt. Craft is out there and he is locked and loaded. He is in the prone position and when you walk out he is going to shoot you!' I told him OK. I said sit down there and have a cup of coffee. I took the helmet liner from him, and his night stick.

I removed my utility shirt so I would look like the 'fire watch' guy. I walked out the back and around the squad bay. And there was Pvt. Craft with an M-16, in the prone position in the middle of the squad bay. I approached him and hit him across the head with the night stick and knocked him out," he said describing the incident as if he had just swatted a fly. To me, this shows how focused and cool a Marine can be under the worst circumstances. Don't forget this guy was laying in wait and planning on shooting Lee.

"After that everybody came waltzing in and subdued him. They took him away in a straight jacket," Lee stated.

I asked Lee what had happened to the private after that. "I don't know. I never saw him again and I never heard of him again," he replied. "That's the story on Pvt. Craft!"

I can't but help to think what had happened if the fire watch had not come in with the warning. I know I wouldn't be here interviewing Lee Weber and that he would not have retired as a 1stSgt. from the Marine Corps.

FRIENDLY FIRE???

Retired Msgt. Les Kenny wasn't afraid when he goofed up. "I was at Parris Island and my troops were up on the third deck. I had this one big kid that was screwing up something terrible. So these recruits had to come running upstairs with their sea bags. This kid gets up there and I stopped him. I said, 'Pvt. your sea bag is down on the deck, go get it!' He went running down the stairs hoisted up his bag and ran back up. He got up there and the bag went flying over the railing again," Les laughed as he related the tale. "It was about 105 degrees that day in PI. By the time he made his fifth trip, he was ready to collapse. I was going to do it one more time. I tossed the bag over the railing and, whoops, there was another private coming out of the barracks. He went flat to the deck. The ambulance came and took him to sick bay. I was filling out papers all week-end after that incident."

My guess is that there should have been somebody down there yelling "incoming" that way everybody else would have run for cover.

ATTITUDE ADJUSTMENT

Les Kenny wanted to talk about one of his favorite Marines, a kid that made him proud. "I picked up Pvt. Greene from receiving. Jesus, what a guy! Long hair, earring, the hole package with a terrible attitude to boot. I thought for sure he was going to be DAB (depot attitude boy). I thought we were going to discharge him right away," he said seriously.

"So the next day I'm out screaming at the platoon for something while they are trying to make a formation and the next thing I knew a canteen goes flying by my smokey. I thought to myself I don't believe this shit!" the former D.I. explained. I could see the fire starting up in Les as he continued with the story.

"I walked over to this asshole and started to remove my duty belt, my shirt, and rank…I was an E-5 at the time. I told him 'Come here, mother fucker, you're gonna' get yours.' Pvt. Greene said no way, he wasn't going to the brig for hitting me. I told him without my stuff on I was a private just like him.

Nothing was going to happen other than my kicking the shit out of him. We went outside and beat the shit out of each other. Thank God I got the upper hand, then I nearly beat him half to death. Then I threw his ass back in the squad bay deck and told everybody to hit the rack for the night." Les paused. It was like he was reliving this event. There was fire in his eyes and a fierceness in his voice.

"The next day I went outside for the morning formation and there was Greene holding the guidon. I walked over to

him and said, 'Scum bag, what are you doing holding that guidon?' He told me he was the new platoon leader. I told him to get his ass back in formation and to give the guidon to the old leader or I would beat his ass again! He complied," said Les after taking a deep breath. He was getting tired because he was so into the story.

A smile now came across the retired Msgt's face. "After some 77 days Pvt. Greene had become my platoon leader. He earned it. He became my dress blues Honor Man," said Les.

"I'm sitting there at graduation…and this guy is standing there, a Navy Chief, decked out in his dress blues. This guy had more gold hash marks on his sleeve than I've ever seen. He came over and asked if I was Sgt. Kenny, I replied that I was. Then he wanted to give me a bottle of Black Velvet. No way! To accept a gratuity was like signing your death warrant," he informed me.

"I told the chief there was no way I could accept that gift. Then the chief told me, 'Sgt., you're only an E-5, Dude, I'm an E-8, you're gonna' take this booze.' Then he asked me how badly I beat the shit out of his son. I asked who his son was and he told me it was Pvt. Greene," Les said laughing. "He said I must have really beat the shit out of him because when he left home he was a piece of shit. The kid joined the Marine Corps just to piss off the old man."

I GET A KICK OUT OF YOU!

E veryone likes to be given a show of confidence once in awhile. Some times it takes longer than we expect. For Lee Weber that was the case. "I was with my first platoon as a junior D.I. We had to get ready for the final inspection so we hung poncho covers over the windows to black out the lights. We were not allowed to have lights on after a certain hour. We had to stay up to get ready for this inspection. I had these guys up into the wee hours polishing, spit shining, cleaning weapons, and swabbing the deck. We didn't miss a thing," Lee explained.

"The following night, after the inspection, I had the duty. The senior drill instructor, Sgt. Shyrock, informed me that we had flunked the inspection. He told me to bring them to the pits. So I marched them over to the sand pits in their full greens and worked the shit out of them. These recruits were worn out," Lee said to me.

"Then I got them back in the barracks. I told them to move the racks to the side. 'Ladies, you are going to pay for that inspection!' Then I commenced to P.T. the hell out of them right in the barracks. One of the privates came up to me and told me he was on light duty. I told him bull shit! Get back out there and P.T. I had the platoon secretary get the medical records to see what was what. I looked up and saw this guy on his stomach instead of doing push ups. So I walked up to him and he raised up like he was doing the push up. I kicked him right in the chest…I mean I kicked him hard! He stayed on the ground. Then the secretary came up to me and said, 'Sir, don't look back at the window, but there is a two star General, a Sergeant Major, and a Captain looking in the window.' Of course I couldn't resist, I turned and there was General Fagan looking through the window with all his aides. I went after the private and started to scream that he embarrassed me, the Commanding General, etc., etc. I told him he better get his barracks squared away," he paused to catch a breath. "I thought the General was going to come around the back door and relieve me on the spot."

Obviously, that didn't happen because Lee was here telling this story after he had retired. "Nothing ever happened. Then about ten years later I was the Recon Career Liaison, Career Planner for the 1st Marine Division. I was working for General Fagan. He would always tell me what a fine job I'm doing. Then one day my wife and I are going to the graduation ceremony at San Diego and I see the General. I saluted him and then asked him a question. 'Sir, in your time here at the base did you ever see a D.I. kick a recruit?' He responded that he had. I explained to him that it was me he saw. I asked him why he did not reprimand me at the time. 'Sgt., were you doing your job?' he asked me. I told him I was. Then he said that there was no reason for me to have been reprimanded. He was Old Corps," said Lee with a smile. The fact that General Fagan was the last World War II active duty Marine had impressed Lee.

ON THE JOB TRAINING?

"One of the strangest stories I had ever heard from other D.I.s comes out of San Diego. It's a known fact that third phase Marines will do absolutely anything they are told to do. They are gung ho and just days from graduation. Apparently, a D.I. came out of the mess hall and told his troops to get in the Dempsy Dumpster. He was just screwing with them, but they were well-trained and followed his orders to a tee. There were eighty recruits in the dumpster. The D.I. returned to find the dumpster not there anymore," said Lee with a laugh.

"Needless to say he was very concerned as to where his troops went. So he found out that the truck company came in and hauled it off to MTC, where they dump the garbage," Lee stated.

"The drill instructor, along with the M.P.s caught the truck on the road about a mile away and flagged the driver down. They informed the driver that he had a truck full of eighty bodies that they needed back. From that point they hauled the recruits out and marched them back to the base," Lee chuckled.

DON'T JUST HANG AROUND.....
DO SOMETHING!

Over the years Les Kenney and Lee Weber had shared so many stories that they had to stop to remember just which one of them had been a part of the story. Once it was determined that it was Lee, he finished it up.

"This incident happened in my series but not my platoon. The drill instructor was 'Mad Dog Wright.' Apparently he had caught this one private sitting on the shitter almost every night around two or two-thirty. So he decided to punish the boot. He crucified him," Lee said with a faint smile. I thought to myself this is one I won't hear too often.

"So 'Mad Dog' made the private put his utility jacket on. After it was on he stuck a broom stick through the arms…from one side to the other. Then he hung him up with one end of the broom on one locker and the other end on the other locker. He was hanging like Christ. He left him like that over night," said Lee.

"Early in the morning, the Commanding General had taken one of his surprise visits around the barracks. When he walked through the hall he saw this private hanging there," Lee informed us at the table. "For that incident, it is my understanding that 'Mad Dog' got discharged and spent five years in Leavenworth."

A QUICK THINKING MARINE

The nice thing about interviewing two friends, like Les and Lee, is that if one of them forgets his own story the other guy is there to remind him about it. This probably happens because each guy has heard the other guy's story numerous times.

It happened with this story. We were wrapping up the night and there was a lull as the guys ordered more beer. Les Kenny reminded his old D.I. friend of a story. "Tell him about 'Locker Box Jones!'" Les excitedly told his pal…and Lee picked it up from there.

"Okay," Lee said as his mind searched for details and circumstances from years ago. "I was with the 7th Marines. I was the Radio Chief with them. There was this old crusty Gunny Sgt. named 'Locker Box Jones.'"

For the uneducated I should let you know Lee is going to be referring to the recruit's foot lockers. Foot lockers are wooden boxes that sit at both ends of a rack (bed). Each recruit has one. It keeps pretty much everything he owns in the world, from writing material to uniforms, boots, shoes, underwear, and toiletries. Everything except the clothes he is wearing. The recruit also uses it as a table to write letters on as well as a place to sit while cleaning his rifle in the barracks and spit shine his boots. The dimensions of the wooden box are approximately two-by-three-feet and stand two feet high. I don't know the weight, but trust me when I say they get heavy. And I must add (at least when I was in), they were painted Marine Corps Green!

"'Locker Box Jones' was pissed at the recruits for something so he decided to have them do up and arms, shoulders. That's were you have to hoist the foot locker up to your shoulders, over your head and up in the air," 1stSgt Weber said with a laugh.

Most D.I.s know that this is an extremely difficult task for the privates to do unless they are exceptionally strong…at least to do it for any length of time. And, there is a risk factor. The recruit can have the locker fall back down on top of himself and get knocked out of training or worse yet, he could drop on another recruit by accident. It's the kind of thing that brass knows goes on, but unless they see it they aren't going to get on the D.I.'s case.

"So Jones has the entire platoon standing in the barracks with their foot lockers over their heads. Jones looks to the side and there was the Commanding General looking at the platoon," said Lee with a grin knowing what was coming next.

"So the quick thinking 'Locker Box Jones'" says to his troops, 'OK…now that you have inspected the bottoms of your lockers, ladies, put them down on the deck and inspect the top of your lockers.' 'Foot Locker Jones' beat the system everytime!" laughed Lee.

One more important fact about foot lockers. They take the blame for every black eye, fat lip, and stream of blood found on a recruit in Marine Corp boot camp. Why, there should be an entire section of the brig set aside for foot lockers.

HE WORKED IN THE LAND OF "OZ"?

Lee had just graduated from D.I. school in San Diego. That very afternoon he picked up a phase three platoon. He had gone to the airport to pick the recruits up. The first thing the recruits do, after getting their heads shaved, is fill out questionnaires. Supposedly, this is to get all the pertinent information and background on the newcomers. In reality, I found out, it is to find out who might be a VIP or who is related to a VIP. "This is so we know whose ass we should kick and whose ass gets spared," roared Les.

"Who to beat and who not to beat!" chimed in Lee. "So that evening I was reading the sheets and I came to one where it listed the civilian occupation. I could believe this was real…it said, I painted the yeller line."

"Later I called this recruit, who wrote the job description, into the duty office. 'Are you fuckn' with me private," I yelled at him. He said no Sir. I asked him what the hell did you do before you joined the Marine Corps?" Lee said managing to get out the rest of the story without laughing his head off.

"Sir," the recruit answered in a southern drawl, "I painted the yeller line!"

"'Your fucking with me Pvt.!' I said to him. 'Don't fuck with me, boy,' I screamed at him," said Lee with Les breaking up at the table.

"Sir, has the drill instructor ever driven a car?" the recruit asked oblivious to the situation he was in. Lee said he answered that he had driven a car. The private then asked him if he had driven a car on the road. Lee said he responded that he had in fact driven his car on the road. "Well, Sir," the private responded in all seriousness, "I painted the yeller line on the road."

The people in the restaurant were staring at the three of us as we went into fits of laughter. I laughed so hard at the story my eyes were tearing. The waitress probably thought it was the Mexican food making my eyes water so hard.

I can't thank these two guys enough for all their great tales and the laughs we had. I couldn't have asked for more. Les Kenny and Lee Weber were more than accommodating. This book would not have been complete without some input from some bad-ass D.I.s. When anybody thinks of the Marine Corps......they immediately get a picture of the rock-jawed, invincible D.I.